"I'm telling it the way it [...] *"You're as possessive as e* [...] *you want some whey-faced little mouse who* [...] *a thought of her own . . ."* Her words trailed off.

She was stunned to recognize the sheer panic in her voice, the utter nonsense of what she was saying. T.J. stood, walked over to her, and pulled her into his arms.

"T.J., why don't you hate me? I'm impossible! You can't want to put up with all my—"

"Shh," he interrupted, looking at her with a tender smile. "I finally get it, babe. You're running scared. You'd lost some of your autonomy when you let me get close, and you panicked. You're trying to push me away to a safe distance. But it's not going to work."

"I have no idea what you're talking about," Stefanie protested.

"You're smart enough to figure it out," he said, capturing her mouth, his lips moving gently over hers, gradually increasing their demands until her resistance began dissolving, her body softening, her arms winding around his neck.

She lost all sense of time and place as T.J.'s warmth flowed into her, his kisses driving out her fears. But still she fought giving in to the pleasure. "But I don't want to let you affect me this way."

"You don't have any choice," he answered softly. "Neither do I." Then he crushed her mouth under his without mercy. . . .

WHAT ARE *LOVESWEPT* ROMANCES?

They are stories of true romance and touching emotion. We believe those two very important ingredients are constants in our highly sensual and very believable stories in the *LOVESWEPT* line. Our goal is to give you, the reader, stories of consistently high quality that may sometimes make you laugh, sometimes make you cry, but are always fresh and creative and contain many delightful surprises within their pages.

Most romance fans read an enormous number of books. Those they truly love, they keep. Others may be traded with friends and soon forgotten. We hope that each *LOVESWEPT* romance will be a treasure—a "keeper." We will always try to publish

LOVE STORIES YOU'LL NEVER FORGET
BY AUTHORS YOU'LL ALWAYS REMEMBER

The Editors

LOVESWEPT® • 361

Gail Douglas
The Dreamweavers:
Gambling Lady

BANTAM BOOKS
NEW YORK • TORONTO • LONDON • SYDNEY • AUCKLAND

GAMBLING LADY

A Bantam Book / November 1989

Published simultaneously in the United States and Canada

---

*Bantam Books are published by Bantam Books, a division
of Bantam Doubleday Dell Publishing Group, Inc. Its trademark, consisting of the words "Bantam Books" and the
portrayal of a rooster, is Registered in U.S. Patent and
Trademark Office and in other countries. Marca Registrada.
Bantam Books, 666 Fifth Avenue, New York, New York 10103.*

PRINTED IN THE UNITED STATES OF AMERICA

O   0 9 8 7 6 5 4 3 2 1

To the kid from Sinterville,
for gambling on us.

One

I will not cry, Stefanie repeated to herself through-out the ceremony. *Not one single tear. I won't give him the satisfaction.*

But she did cry, and as more than one willful tear defied Stefanie Sinclair's usual control, she desper-ately clung to the fiction that she was weeping purely from happiness. After all, she thought, very few of the other guests at the wedding were dry-eyed. The joy the bride and groom were radiating had touched every heart.

Yet each poignant phrase of the ceremony was like a knife aimed straight at Stefanie's heart.

She stole a sidelong glance at T.J. Carriere, seated next to her. Had it been almost a year since she'd stood before a justice of the peace with T.J., seeing the same adoration in his gaze that her soon-to-be brother-in-law Cole Jameson was bestowing on her sister Morgan?

And had it been only six months since she'd seen T.J.'s adoration turn to contempt?

She wouldn't think about it! Stefanie decided. What was done couldn't be changed. Morgan deserved better on her special day than to have her sister indulging in useless regrets and sloppy sentimentality. And there was no need to let T.J. know that his impact on her, the supposedly cool, self-possessed, independent Stefanie Sinclair, was as devastating as ever.

But why, oh why, hadn't she discouraged Morgan from inviting T.J. to the wedding, no matter how fond Morgan was of her brother-in-law? And, Stefanie silently berated herself, why had she agreed to sit next to T.J. for appearances' sake? There were times when her stiff-necked pride amounted to out-and-out masochism.

The folding chairs that had been set up in Cole's lovely garden were crowded together to accommodate the many guests, so Stefanie was suffering two annoying indignities: Not only did her glance sneak toward T.J. with infuriating regularity, but her body kept listing to the left as well, like a sinking ship, trying to lean away from him so his shoulder wasn't pressed against hers, so the clean, spicy scent of him wasn't permeating every breath she took, so his warmth wasn't pervading her whole being and triggering rushes of unwelcome memories.

The worst thing was that T.J. knew how uncomfortable she was, Stefanie thought angrily. His smug expression was evidence enough that he was aware of her weakness and enjoyed it.

No sooner had she formed the silent accusation than her innate sense of fairness made her take it back. T.J. was not a smug man. He wouldn't take pleasure from anyone's discomfort. Not even hers.

The fact that she could be so unjust bothered Stefanie. Why was she fabricating faults for T.J.?

Didn't he have enough real ones? And, if she really wanted to be honest, hadn't *she* been the real culprit in the failure of their marriage?

The minister's voice broke into her troubled thoughts. "Will you, Cole, take Morgan to be your . . ."

Blinking rapidly, lifting her chin, and forcing a tiny smile, Stefanie battled waves of nostalgia, concentrating instead on how lovely Morgan looked, her golden hair a soft halo of curls, her eyes shining with love for the man to whose destiny she was joining hers.

Stefanie was delighted with her new brother-in-law. Cole Jameson was so right for Morgan, it was almost eerie—as her sister Heather was ready to point out at every turn. With a fond glance at the youngest Sinclair sister, Morgan's only bridal attendant, Stefanie grew steadier and smiled.

Heather was enjoying her I-told-you-so moment. The ultimate romantic, she believed in soul mates, in predestined partners, and in happy endings. And it did seem that the little minx was right, at least where Morgan and Cole were concerned.

But Heather wasn't right about her oldest sister and T.J. Carriere, Stefanie thought, her smile fading. All the faith and wishes in the world couldn't conjure up a happy ending for their particular love story. It was over.

She stifled a sigh, wishing T.J. weren't so appealing, with his unruly chestnut hair, his crooked grin, his expressive green eyes. Did he have to be so tall and well built, so dashing in his European-cut blue suit? Must he look like such an intriguing Cajun rogue?

Desperate to stop dwelling on T.J.'s charms,

Stefanie forced herself to pay attention to her surroundings, but even that was a mistake. The garden behind Cole's Key West mansion was like a miniature Eden, adorned and perfumed with poinciana, hibiscus, and frangipani, sheltered on every side by a wall of greenery, thickly carpeted with lush, soft grass, and studded at the center by an aquamarine pool.

It was all reminiscent of a certain honeymoon hideaway in Jamaica, Stefanie recalled dreamily, unable to suppress the insistent mental images that had plagued her for six lonely months. If only . . .

Abruptly, she pulled herself together, deciding that she'd wasted far too much time on *if only*'s. She'd come to Key West to celebrate the beginning of her sister's marriage not to mourn the end of her own.

Gentle laughter rippled through the small group of guests, drawing Stefanie's attention back to the ceremony.

"What happened?" she whispered to T.J. before she recalled that she hadn't intended to speak to her husband if she could avoid it.

T.J. turned to Stefanie in slight surprise, wondering why she hadn't noticed that the minister, obviously coached by Cole, had ended the ceremony with the announcement that the bride could kiss the groom. It was a playful reversal of tradition Stefanie should have appreciated. "Where were your thoughts, babe?" T.J. asked softly.

Stefanie melted for just an instant, then straightened her backbone. Babe, she thought. Pet names came too easily to T.J. Carriere. And if there was one name that didn't suit Stefanie Sinclair, it was *babe.* "I was thinking about—about the caterers," she mumbled.

T.J. smiled as he looked away. Not for a moment did he believe Stefanie. He'd been married to her for only a few months, and theirs had been a whirlwind courtship of just over three weeks, but he could read her well enough to know her mind hadn't been on the caterers. The direction of her gaze and the tell-tale moisture in her eyes suggested that her thoughts had been with his, on a Caribbean paradise very much like this Key West Shangri-la.

He allowed himself a brief glance at his estranged wife, then looked away again, longing to return to the days when he could drink in her loveliness as much as he liked, perhaps even reach out to smooth back the silken fall of her honey-blond hair, watch the soft gray of her eyes darken with passion, trace the strong but exquisite features that were burned into his memory like a brand.

He suppressed another smile, amused by the impassive mask Stefanie always wore—*almost* always, he corrected himself, vividly recalling the many times and ways he'd seen her lower it to reveal the real woman underneath.

He couldn't resist taking yet another glance at her. Even wearing a fragile-looking dress of rose silk—his favorite color on her—Stefanie exuded strength. Her special brand of womanly power challenged and excited T.J. on countless levels. It also aroused vivid memories that drove him wild: The athletic yet feminine tautness of her muscles, the firm ripeness of her breasts, the smooth satin of her thighs. A mental picture assailed him of Stefanie straddling him, her eyes glazed with pleasure, her body arched as she took what she wanted—and what he gave so willingly. A familiar ache spread through his body as he recalled the warmth of her enfolding him, surrounding him. . . .

The film of moisture that broke out on his forehead warned T.J. that he was letting his thoughts wander into dangerous territory. With a determined effort, he returned his attention to his sister-in-law's wedding, sincerely rejoicing in the fact that Morgan had found a man like Cole Jameson to treasure her as she deserved to be treasured. Morgan occupied a special spot in T.J.'s heart, though he was deeply attached to all the Sinclairs. Heather was like Morgan; ingenuous and open and full of beans. Lisa, seated to T.J.'s right, was more like Stefanie in looks and temperament: subdued, elegant, controlled.

His thoughts and his gaze inevitably found their way back to his wife. It was fitting, he mused with a tiny smile, that Stefanie was president of Dreamweavers, Inc., the phenomenally successful travel company founded by the four sisters. T.J. thought the name described Stefanie perfectly. Without even trying, she'd woven dreams that had haunted him from the first moment he'd seen her, dreams that would stay with him forever, he was certain.

The wedding ceremony was almost over, he realized as the guitarist—a local street musician Cole and Morgan had hired for the occasion—began a stately, traditional wedding recessional.

The music released a flood of nostalgia in T.J. that was more than he could control. Hardly aware of what he was doing, he reached out to curl his fingers around Stefanie's hands as they lay tightly clasped in her lap. "Hey, babe," he whispered, his throat constricted with emotion, "they're playing our song."

The heat of T.J.'s touch, the telltale rasp in his voice, the sweetness of his words were almost too much for Stefanie. She bit down on her lower lip hard enough to stifle a sob, but couldn't keep another stream of uncharacteristic tears from squeezing past her closed eyelids. She extricated her hands from T.J.'s gentle grasp and dug into her purse, horrified to discover she'd forgotten tissues.

Seeing her dilemma, T.J. started patting his suit pockets, feeling guilty. The last thing he'd wanted to do was upset Stefanie, and he didn't have a handkerchief to offer her. What kind of husband was he, anyway?

To his relief, Lisa took a small packet of tissues from her purse and handed them to him with a wink and a smile. As T.J. passed the packet on to Stefanie, he mused sadly that her whole family seemed to want him back in the fold. They trusted him, believed in him. Why couldn't she?

Stefanie was relieved to have the tissues but angry with herself. She had to stop letting her feelings run amok. It wasn't at all like her to be self-indulgent—at least not in public.

As the guests rose to applaud the happy couple coming down the makeshift aisle, Stefanie stood and vowed to get hold of herself. She tried a concentration game, mentally listing the presidents. It was too easy. She tried vice presidents: John Adams, Thomas Jefferson, Aaron Burr . . . To her disbelief and irritation, she was stuck before she'd gotten a good running start, though she'd mastered the list ages ago. She started over: Adams, Jefferson, Burr . . .

T.J. leaned toward her with a devilish smile and spoke softly. "George Clinton."

She stared at him. "I beg your pardon?"

"George Clinton was Jefferson's vice president after Aaron Burr."

Stefanie was amazed that T.J. had remembered her silly game, let alone had guessed that she was using it at this very moment. He'd even pinpointed exactly where she'd been stumped! Curiosity got the best of her. "How did you know?" she whispered.

T.J. grinned. "I guess you don't remember admitting to me that whenever you were . . . upset . . . you got stuck after Aaron Burr. And it made you twice as mad as you were to begin with. A certain look comes over your face, babe."

At that moment, the guitarist switched into an intricate jazz version of the wedding recessional, and the guests took the upbeat tempo as a signal that the formalities of the wedding were over.

Reeling from the knowledge that T.J. had read her mind as if there were no emotional chasm between them, Stefanie pasted on a bright smile for Morgan's sake, and moved away from him.

T.J. was disappointed but not surprised.

Lisa startled him by standing on tiptoe to kiss his cheek. "Steffie's worth a battle, T.J., and so are you. That's why Morgan has been playing the matchmaker, and the rest of us are cooperating."

Bemused, T.J. stared after Lisa as she went to hug Morgan and Cole. What did she mean by that cryptic remark? He'd been invited to the wedding to give him a chance to be close to Stefanie? Or was Morgan up to something more? He hoped so. He hadn't expected his second conquest of Stefanie Sinclair to be as straightforward as the first. He was prepared to fight for her, but he would take all the help he could get.

From the instant he'd first laid eyes on Stefanie, just over a year earlier, he'd known with uncanny certainty that she was going to be important in his life.

He'd been fascinated by her, by the cool surface that hid her fiery nature, by the contrast between the inner Stefanie and the person she presented to the world.

Despite the heartache he'd endured over the last six months, T.J. knew that if the clock were turned back to the time of his initial encounter with Stefanie, he would pursue her with the same single-minded determination he'd shown then—and intended to show now.

Assigned by a science magazine to cover a well-organized toxic-waste protest, where Stefanie had been a speaker, T.J. had been moved so deeply by the fervor of her plea for environmental awareness, he'd been hard put to give his attention to the remainder of the rally. He'd decided he had to meet her, had to know her.

The need for some personal quotes to add depth to his magazine piece had been his excuse for seeking her out, and by the end of the interview he'd fallen hard for Stefanie Sinclair. She was everything he admired: articulate, intelligent, committed to the causes she'd made her own, and, as a bonus, utterly lovely.

Magnificently tall, her bearing regal, her manner assertive and straightforward, Stefanie was slightly intimidating. But T.J. had refused to be intimidated.

Convinced that he'd glimpsed a deliciously feminine, down-to-earth, passionate woman under her polished veneer, he'd treated her accordingly. He'd taken her to his favorite New Orleans haunts—rarely the trendy and exclusive places—and had come up with off-beat, simple pleasures he'd suspected she would enjoy.

And Stefanie had responded to him. Instantly. Profoundly. Love and need and desire hadn't grown between them at an easy, comfortable pace. Everything had exploded at once.

For T.J., it still was exploding, even after all that had gone wrong. Privately, he renewed the marriage vows he and Stefanie had exchanged. For better, for worse, she was his, and he was hers. All he had to do was make her realize that fact, admit it, and live by it.

Stefanie managed to avoid T.J. during the champagne toasts and the buffet, but she was startled to find him at her elbow just as Morgan tossed her bouquet.

"Maybe we should have had a wedding like this instead of our impulsive elopement," he said, handing her a fresh glass of champagne. "It's nice, isn't it?"

Stefanie was tempted to refuse the drink but didn't want to seem churlish, so she accepted it after putting down her empty glass. "It seems we shouldn't have had a wedding at all," she answered in a strained voice.

At first T.J. was hurt by the remark, then he saw the pain in Stefanie's eyes. Lost for words, he was almost grateful when he and Stefanie were approached by a slim, white-haired woman in a stylish blue dress. She held out her hand to Stefanie. "Stefanie, I can't tell you how pleased I am that your sister has become my daughter-in-law. She's such a lovely girl."

"Hi, Mrs. Jameson," Stefanie said around the lump in her throat. She grasped the older woman's hand. "I'm glad you feel that way about Morgan. Perhaps I'm a bit prejudiced, but I think she's pretty special too. And I happen to know that she's delighted with her new family."

"How do you do, Mrs. Jameson," T.J. said with a touch of uncharacteristic awkwardness, shifting from one foot to the other, wondering how he and Stefanie should handle their first social encounter since their separation.

"Hello," Mrs. Jameson answered with a pleasant smile. "Are you one of Cole's friends?"

T.J. grinned, deciding to state his position literally, if not with total accuracy. "The fact is, I'm your son's brother-in-law, as of a few minutes ago." He thrust out his hand to grasp hers. "Sorry I arrived too late to meet you and Mr. Jameson before the ceremony. I'm T.J. Carriere. Stefanie's husband." He liked saying those words. Somehow, he would make them mean something again. Silently, he dared Stefanie to deny them.

Mrs. Jameson looked quizzically at Stefanie. "I gather you kept your maiden name when you married, the way so many young people are doing?"

Stefanie nodded. It was true, so she wasn't lying by neglecting to tell Mrs. Jameson that she and T.J. were separated.

The older woman studied T.J. closely. "Then you were the one Morgan went with to that Central American rain forest to get her parents out of some dreadful little jail?"

Nodding, T.J. avoided looking at Stefanie. He knew she'd been angry when she'd heard about that particular adventure. "It was a fairly straightforward rescue operation," he said with a strained smile. "A small misunderstanding had to be cleared up, that's all."

Mrs. Jameson laughed and shook her head. "You sound like Morgan."

T.J. saw Stefanie bristle, though she remained silent. He knew eventually he was going to have to answer for leaving her in the dark while turning to Morgan for help, but he'd had his reasons. "As you mentioned, it was an unpleasant jail," he said to Mrs. Jameson, "and Kate and Charlie didn't belong there. As I'm sure Morgan has told you, her parents had staged a legitimate, peaceful protest against the clearing of hundreds of acres of rain forest. The authorities agreed to save the forest once we'd explained things to them."

In spite of her lingering anger at T.J. for deciding to tell Morgan and only Morgan about the trouble her parents had gotten into, Stefanie felt a reluctant rush of admiration for him.

T.J. always seemed to know which buttons to push to accomplish anything, Stefanie had to admit. It was another of his plentiful charms.

"My son seems to have married into quite a colorful family," Mrs. Jameson said, her glance darting between Stefanie and T.J., her forehead creased in a frown. Then she smiled at T.J. and spoke so brightly, it was obvious she was changing the subject deliberately. "What do your initials stand for? Or shouldn't I ask?"

Grateful to the woman for steering the conversation in a safer direction, T.J. answered her innocent question cheerfully. "If you'd asked when I was twenty years younger, I might have balked at telling you. At thirteen, I was sensitive about being called Little John in the schoolyard. My father's name was Jean, and when I was named after him, my relatives naturally called me Ti-Jean, a diminutive for Petit Jean. Thus, the initials."

Stefanie had recovered enough poise to join the conversation, and couldn't resist a mild jibe. "But your name is Jean Philippe. You used the initials of your nickname."

"I guess I just wasn't thinking," T.J. said with feigned embarrassment. Actually, he was delighted that Stefanie was teasing him a little. Light banter had been part of their relationship from the start.

"You're French, then?" Mrs. Jameson asked. "And you're from New Orleans?"

"I'm a Cajun," T.J. answered proudly.

"You don't sound like a Cajun," Mrs. Jameson remarked. "You have a charming sort of drawl—or perhaps twang is a better word—but it's all I can do to understand the Cajun dialect when it's spoken."

T.J. winked at her. "Well, now, ah'm jes' as Cajun as can be, ma'am, I gar-awn-tee!"

Stefanie laughed with Mrs. Jameson at T.J.'s outlandish accent. He could be so maddeningly adorable when he chose. "Excuse me," she murmured, suddenly desperate to escape him. "I should go help Morgan get changed. She and Cole are ready to leave on their honeymoon."

Mrs. Jameson nodded and smiled quizzically, again obviously aware of the tension between them. "I'm sure your T.J. and I will find lots to talk about, dear," she said as Stefanie walked away.

He's not my T.J.! Stefanie wanted to protest, but there was no point putting a damper on anyone's mood. The following day she'd say good-bye to T.J. once again, return to New Orleans, and then the recovery process could begin anew.

The party seemed interminable. Stefanie was relieved when the last guests had left and only the immediate Sinclair and Jameson families remained.

"I'll drop you at your hotel," T.J. said, cupping his hand under Stefanie's elbow after she'd wished the others good night and was ready to be on her way.

"I can take a cab, thank you," she answered quietly, hating the way T.J. could make her tremble inside.

"I mean in a cab, babe. Where are you staying?"

Stefanie knew T.J. well enough to realize that if he'd decided to see her back to her hotel, he would do it regardless of her objections, embarrassing her if necessary. His insistent nature was one of the many reasons she and T.J. hadn't made a go of their marriage. For all his gentle Southern charm, he could act like a domineering redneck.

Her family was of no help, Stefanie thought with a touch of annoyance. Every single one of the Sinclairs had made a point of showing T.J. how much he was accepted as part of the clan.

For the moment, Stefanie saw little recourse but to give in. "Morgan booked me into the Pier House," she told T.J., then noticed that he was looking at her with an amused expression. She arched her brow. "Did I say something humorous?"

T.J. shook his head, still smiling at the realization that Morgan had been very thoughtful about the hotel bookings. "No, darlin'. Just something interesting, that's all." Releasing Stefanie's elbow, he casually placed his hand on the small of her back, at the same time waving to the remaining family members. "See you for breakfast," he said, then began guiding Stefanie along the stone walkway to the front yard.

"Breakfast?" Stefanie repeated, realizing that she should have known her parents and sisters would invite T.J. to join them for a farewell get-together in the morning. "I have the feeling I'm being led down the garden path. Literally and figuratively," she muttered, wishing her body would stop responding to T.J.'s every touch.

"Hey, babe, I'm still family, remember?" he said with feigned confidence. When they reached the street, he paused. "The Pier House isn't far from here. How about walking?"

Stefanie frowned. T.J. was right. The hotel wasn't far enough to rate a cab ride. Yet she was wary of strolling with him under banyan trees and a cloudless, glittering night sky. The sea air and tropical blooms were mingling with T.J.'s own special fragrance to tantalize her senses, and his soft, persuasive voice had a way of lulling her into a dangerous dreamy state.

"What's the matter?" he asked. "Don't you trust yourself to be alone with me?"

Stefanie glared at him and began striding in the direction of the hotel. "I'd trust myself to be alone with you on a deserted island for a year, Jean Philippe Carriere."

He grinned. "How much do you want to bet?"

"That's one wager I'll pass on, thank you."

"That in itself says it all," T.J. commented, glad

he had long legs and was in good shape. Keeping up with a Sinclair woman in a hurry, especially Stefanie, could be a challenge. "I've never known you to turn down any bet, unless you knew for certain you'd lose."

Stefanie clamped her lips together, refusing to dignify his remark with an answer. He was right, but she wasn't about to admit it.

Swinging her arms as she walked, Stefanie wondered why T.J. was making things so difficult. She didn't blame him for wanting to attend Morgan's wedding, or even for pretending their marriage was harmonious during the afternoon and evening. But why he was continuing the charade was beyond her.

When they reached the hotel complex, T.J. stayed right with Stefanie. She turned and managed a tiny smile. "I think I'll be fine from here on, thank you."

His eyes widened in mock innocence. "I'm sure you will, honey, but I'd like to get some sleep myself, and since this is also my hotel. . . ."

Stefanie's heart sank, but she said nothing more as T.J. followed her all the way to her room. "Really, T.J.," she said when she stopped at her door. "What's your game?"

His smile was so angelic, Stefanie almost thought she saw a halo over his head. "I have no game, Steffie. I'm just going to my room." He held up his key to show her the number, and grinned when she blanched, confirming his suspicions. "We seem to be neighbors."

"Next-door neighbors," Stefanie said, her pulse beginning to race out of control. "Why, T.J.?"

"Ask your sister. Morgan made the reservations."

"But she put Lisa and Heather in the Marriott . . ." Stefanie's voice trailed off as the truth hit her.

T.J. tried in vain to suppress his pleased grin, despite Stefanie's shock. Now that he knew what Lisa had meant about Morgan's matchmaking, he felt a burst of confidence. Stefanie's whole family must have known what Morgan was up to, and they approved of her efforts. Since none of them would do anything to hurt Stefanie, it was evident they firmly believed this marriage deserved a second chance.

He leaned one hand on the wall beside Stefanie's door and spoke as persuasively as he could. "This place has a great dockside bar, babe. Join me for a nightcap?"

Stefanie fumbled with her key, trying to fit it into the lock. She wanted to refuse the invitation but found herself hesitating. The idea of a quiet drink with T.J. under a tropical moon was as tempting as it was terrifying.

"I'll tell you what," T.J. said as he saw that her resolve was faltering. He took a half dollar from his pocket, one he'd put there for just such a moment. "Since you aren't sure, why don't we let fate decide? Heads you accept, tails you don't."

Stefanie had to smile. T.J. knew her too well; she couldn't resist his wager, even when she was sure he was up to his old tricks. "You're on," she said in a small voice.

T.J. gave the coin a quick flip, slapped it onto the back of his hand, and showed it to Stefanie. "There you go, babe. Heads it is."

With a tiny shrug, Stefanie put her key back into her handbag and nodded. "Who can argue with fate? It appears I'm going for that nightcap," she said softly, wondering why she was giving in when being with T.J. could bring her only more unhappiness.

T.J. pocketed his half dollar, barely suppressing a grin. Stefanie knew about his special two-headed half dollar. As a joke, he'd bought it at a novelty shop just after meeting her and learning about her little gambling quirk.

Stefanie had an excellent memory.

Yet she hadn't asked for a closer look at the coin.

His hopes began to soar.

Two

Seated opposite T.J. at an outdoor table of the dock-side bar, Stefanie knew she'd made a mistake. Sitting with T.J. at the wedding hadn't been punishment enough. Now she was putting herself through a multiple assault on her senses, with a gentle breeze brushing her skin, the mellow riff of a jazz trumpet floating across the water from another waterfront bar, the scent of the ocean in the air, T.J. Carriere by moonlight, and a sky filled with stars winking as if they knew something she didn't.

T.J. ordered Armagnac for her, just as he'd always done, without first asking whether it was what she wanted. Stefanie thought of pointing out to him that her tastes might have changed, but they hadn't, so she let the moment pass. Besides, she believed in saving her ammunition for battles that counted—and she had a distinct feeling that T.J. was gearing up for some kind of skirmish.

She assumed a no-nonsense manner as soon as the waiter had brought the drinks. "What's this about, T.J.?"

Knowing he should have been ready for her blunt question, he bought a little time. "What's what about?"

Stefanie was too straightforward to let him get away with playing dumb. She fixed him with a level gaze. "You know exactly what I mean, so please get to the point."

"All right," he said quietly, deciding to play things her no-nonsense way. "Why aren't we divorced?"

So that was it, Stefanie thought, her stomach contracting as if recoiling from a sharp blow. He wanted a divorce. He'd expected her to take care of the matter.

Suddenly she was furious with herself. Why had she humiliated herself by waiting until he'd had to ask for the divorce? Why had she allowed herself to hope, just a little, that he still cared about her?

Shaking inside but determined to maintain an outward show of dignity, she turned his question back on him. "You tell me. You're the one who walked out. I assumed you would take care of the legalities." It was a stupid thing to say, she realized as soon as she'd spoken the words. T.J. had told her earlier in the day that he'd been out of the States since just after their separation. Naturally, he'd assumed that she had arranged for divorce proceedings.

But she hadn't done a thing, and apparently T.J. wasn't pleased by the oversight. Had he met someone else, someone he wanted to marry?

The thought made Stefanie's insides twist painfully. But she told herself to be sensible. A divorce was inevitable. "I'm sorry, T.J.," she said in a low voice that somehow remained steady. "I've been terribly busy at work, and I simply haven't gotten around to calling a lawyer." With a supreme effort, she even managed a rueful laugh before going on. "I guess filing for divorce is like doing tax returns—easy to put off till tomorrow. But I promise I'll do something about it on Monday. Or you can start the proceedings, if you wish. I won't contest it. I'll try to make it happen as quickly and painlessly as possible. I owe you that much."

T.J. reached for her snifter and curved his palms around the bowl, warming the Armagnac with his own body heat, a habit he'd begun on their very first evening together. "I'm not suggesting you should have arranged for a divorce, baby," he said after a long silence, his voice slightly husky. He handed her the snifter, his fingers lingering for a moment on hers as she accepted it. "I'm only asking why you haven't. And I don't think you've given me an honest answer."

To her dismay, Stefanie's eyes filled with tears again. She took a careful sip of the Armagnac, feeling T.J.'s warmth on the glass and in the smooth, amber liquid that slid down her throat, calming and soothing her. "How many times have I told you not to call me *baby*?" she said. Confused by T.J's response, she feared she might do something unforgivable and ridiculous, like burst into sobs and throw herself into the familiar comfort of his arms. "I'm not the baby type, remember? I don't fit the image. I'm too tall, too bossy, and too . . ." She hesitated, hardly aware of what she was rambling on about, hating the way T.J. could go straight for the emotional jugular.

"You're too independent?" T.J. supplied with a little smile, speaking lightly to hide the depth of his own emotion. "Responsible? Mature?"

"Right," Stefanie said, taking another sip of her drink. "So cut it out, will you? I'm nobody's baby."

"I'll try to remember," he answered, reaching across the table to feather his fingertips over her forearm.

An involuntary shiver of delight passed through Stefanie; she'd always loved T.J.'s gentle touch, his habit of caressing her in an absentminded way whenever they were close. Even during their quiet, companionable moments of reading in bed, T.J. would be absorbed in his book yet stroking her thigh. Watching television, he would reach for her and cuddle her in his arms. Walking down the street, he would rest his palm on her waist, or slide his arm around her shoulders, or hold her hand. To her horror, more tears were stinging her eyelids, threatening to spill over. "Good lord, what on earth's the matter with me?" she asked with another tremulous laugh as she sat back, drawing her arm out of T.J.'s reach. Did he want a divorce or didn't he? "I guess watching the first of my kid sisters get married had more effect on me than I'd anticipated," she said, summoning her considerable willpower to beam a brilliant smile at T.J. and speak with what she hoped was casual cheerfulness. "So what have you been doing besides riding to the rescue when my folks land in jail?"

"I've picked up a few routine magazine assignments," T.J. answered, his guard up instantly, though he made no effort to digress from the issue. "Of course, nothing I'm working on at the moment is as exciting as the piece I did on the destruction of another huge tract of rain forest."

Stefanie's smile turned cool, despite her gratitude to T.J. for being ready and able to help her family when he was needed. "Just how did you happen to be Ti-Jean on the spot when trouble hit Mom and Dad in that remote village anyway?"

T.J. sensed Stefanie's displeasure in her polite question, but he answered as if taking her words at face value. "Charlie called to ask me to fly down and cover a protest against a multinational timber company's bulldozer invasion. He wanted publicity for the rally he and Kate were trying to organize. Fortunately, as things turned out, the corporate idiot who'd paid to have them jailed also came to understand the potential impact of widespread, highly negative publicity."

Stefanie took a deep breath. She didn't relish the idea of fighting with T.J., but she couldn't keep her resentment to herself. She spoke in measured syllables. "Look, T.J., let's get this thing out into the open. Why did you call Morgan to go with you? Why didn't I know anything about it until after the whole mess had been cleared up?"

T.J. was ready with a brutally honest answer. "First, I didn't need any arguments. I'd planned how to accomplish the desired goal, and I knew Morgan would cooperate without trying to run things." As T.J. saw a silver flame of anger in Stefanie's eyes, he put out his hand as if to stop her. "Before you blow your top, babe, admit to yourself that you and I can barely make coffee and toast together without a clash of wills."

Forced to concede the truth of what T.J. was saying, and hurt by his derogatory reference to some of their intimate, morning-after moments, Stefanie pressed her lips together to keep from arguing with him and proving his point.

"Good," he said with a tight smile. "You're going to let me finish. Let's get to the second and more important reason I wanted Morgan along instead of you: I didn't need a distraction. I didn't need to be thinking about our problems instead of the immediate situation. I didn't need to be worrying about you."

"I've trekked through my share of jungles," Stefanie said, unable to remain silent. "There'd have been no need for you to play the protective male in a rain forest with me, any more than with my sister."

T.J. nodded. "I know, babe. But the point is, I . . . well, I lose my sense of proportion where you're concerned. It's not the same with Morgan. Fond as I am of her, I'm not as involved emotionally. Steffie, face it. I can't deny or fight this primitive need of mine to take care of you. That urge is a reality, and maybe it's one of our problems, but the trip to that remote village wasn't the time to deal with it."

Stefanie refused to give in. "Couldn't you have told me what was going on at least? You actually asked Morgan not to call me."

"If you'd been told about the situation, you'd have been there," T.J. said with a smile. "Am I right?"

Stefanie didn't answer for several moments but finally heaved a sigh. "I suppose so." After another long pause she forced herself to add, "Thanks for what you did. I guess we all owe you a lot. Morgan and I would have known where to find our folks, but as usual, I'd have insisted on sticking to the proper diplomatic channels to get them out of jail, and probably they'd be there even now."

"No one owes me anything, and I don't expect thanks," T.J. said flatly, taken aback by Stefanie's statement. At the heart of so many quarrels in their brief marriage had been their different styles of dealing with both personal problems and public issues. Stefanie believed in "proper channels," in negotiation, in quiet but stubborn—sometimes infuriatingly stubborn—persuasion. T.J. was more inclined to be forceful, to battle toe-to-toe, both at home and elsewhere. During the past six months, he'd worked hard at toning down his aggressiveness. Dare he hope that Stefanie had modified her view a little too? That they were finding their way to some sort of middle ground?

He decided to test the waters. "Your family is my family, remember? Not only legally either. I care a lot for Kate and Charlie, and I admire the stand they took in that rain forest. If more people fought against the abuse of the planet, it might not be in such a state of chaos."

Stefanie lapsed into another silence. She was aware that T.J. was edging dangerously close to the cause of their final quarrel, one that had escalated out of control and had helped shatter their marriage. Was he deliberately probing, trying to learn whether she'd changed at all in six months?

Suddenly she was annoyed with him. Hadn't she conceded already that his way had been the right one for the rain forest situation? Hadn't she agreed, more or less, that she'd have impeded him by insisting on doing things her way? What did he want from her? An admission that she was wrong and he was right about everything in the whole damned universe?

She chose to play it safe by agreeing with him in principle. "Sometimes I wonder if the people who deliberately, knowingly pollute and strip the environment are childless and expect to die young. They don't seem to care much about the future, as long as the dollars keep flowing in now."

T.J. looked down, hiding a small grin. Stefanie had avoided giving him the answer he was seeking, and he knew he couldn't push her. He had to be satisfied with the fact that she approved of the way he'd handled the matter of rescuing her parents—which was, when he thought about it, a major concession on her part. The Stefanie he remembered would still be second-guessing his every move.

He took another sip of his drink, then smiled at Stefanie. "By the way, are you still battling that company you were picketing and speaking against at the rally where you and I met? Gardner Chemicals, I believe it was?" He remembered too late that he'd hit on another sore point.

Stefanie wondered if his question was as innocent as it sounded. More than once T.J. had pointed to the chemical firm's unwillingness to clean up its act as a perfect example of why her kind of peaceful tactics rarely achieved anything. Once again she had to concede that he was right. "We're getting absolutely nowhere," she admitted. "Those people just keep dumping and spewing their poisons." Abruptly she changed the subject. "I understand from my father that you spent time in the far north on some sort of undercover assignment."

T.J. was aware that Stefanie was trying to skirt the real issues between them. For the moment, he went along with her, though he hated the constant undercurrents, the conversations that were more focused on what wasn't said than what was. "A wildlife magazine asked me to go undercover as a poacher, believe it or not. So off I went to the land of the midnight sun for a few weeks and got my first-person story on the wholesale slaughter of bears and the worldwide selling of various products on the black market. It wasn't the most pleasant job I've had to do, but the exposé will hit the stands in a couple of months, and the poachers are in jail, so it was worthwhile."

Stefanie felt the blood drain from her face. "Weren't you in danger?"

T.J. was reluctant to dwell on the experience. He'd despised the ruse he'd been a part of, even if he'd done it for a worthwhile reason. "I suppose I could have run into trouble, though the threat I felt most on a day-to-day basis was the possibility of losing my mind out of sheer boredom. As you can imagine, I didn't have a whole lot in common with the other men, and nights in the northern wilderness are long. On the other hand, I had time to do some clear thinking."

Stefanie refused to be drawn into a discussion of what T.J. had thought about during those nights. His mind no doubt had wandered into the regions where hers had been, probably on the same nights. . . . "What's next on your agenda?"

T.J. was amazed. He'd never seen Stefanie so skittish. Normally, she was a woman who faced every issue head-on. "I'm planning a few easy projects," he answered. "I'm even hoping to get away from the constant, depressing grind of writing about things like environmental problems and endangered species in favor of something more upbeat. And I don't need any more adventures for a while."

"You mean T.J. Carriere is going to indulge in some rest and recreation away from the field of battle at last?"

" 'Fraid so," he answered with a grin. "I'm getting too old to keep trying to police the world."

Stefanie found herself smiling back at him. "I suppose the day of the desk job arrives for everyone, even you. Why, I can hear your ancient bones creaking even as we sit here. Isn't it sad the way men start into a decline at—how old are you now? all of thirty-three?" She clicked her tongue. "Positively decrepit, poor thing."

T.J. threw back his head and laughed, pleased to see a flash of the Stefanie who never had been able to resist kidding him. "Now you know my secret. I need someone to take care of me in my old age. That's why I want my wife back."

Stiffening, Stefanie gaped at him. "What did you say?"

"Just what you thought I said," T.J. replied gravely. "Not only am I glad there's no divorce in the works, I hope there never will be. I want us to try again, Steffie."

Stefanie stared into the depths of her brandy snifter, then raised it to her lips and downed all that remained of its contents. "You know what an exercise in futility a reconciliation between us would be," she said after several moments. "I think you're reacting to the sentiment of Morgan's wedding." She put down the glass. "I also think I should be getting back to my room now. I have to pack. I'll be leaving on the commuter flight to Miami right after breakfast with the family."

T.J. had been ready for her reaction, so when she started to rise, his hand snaked out to curl around her wrist and tug her back into her chair. "There's no sense running, babe. I'll just catch up."

There was no sense fighting, either, Stefanie thought as she sat down again, glad there wasn't anyone at the nearby tables to see the embarrassing little scene. She hated public spectacles, and T.J. knew it. Direct, forceful action was still his style.

She shot him a look of sheer desperation. "Why

would you say these things? You walked out on me six months ago, and I didn't see you or hear from you until today. Now you're telling me you want me back, and I'm supposed to welcome you as if nothing has happened?" She heard her voice rising, felt her dignity slipping away. When she spoke again, it was with controlled calm. "Look, I admit I was devastated for a while, but I've been doing a pretty fair job of getting over you, and I don't plan to invite a relapse at this stage of the game." Glaring at the hand that manacled her wrist, she tried another tack. "Do I need to point out that there are deeper issues between us than philosophical arguments?"

"Just tell me this much," T.J. said very quietly. "Did you believe I was capable of the things you accused me of that day when I got back from San Francisco? More to the point, do you believe any of it now that you've had time to think?"

Unable to look at him, Stefanie hesitated. She wasn't sure herself how much she'd meant and how many of her awful words had been born out of some inexplicable panic. "You didn't deny that you'd been involved in scuttling the tuna boat," she said at last.

"I didn't deny it because I was more than involved in scuttling that boat," T.J. said, glad of the chance to tell his side of the story at last. "In fact, I take full credit for the job."

"What?" Stefanie said softly, shocked. "But I—I thought you . . ." She had to pause to catch her breath, as if the wind had been knocked out of her. "You admit you did it, yet you were furious about my fleeting suspicions? How dare you sit there and—"

"I scuttled the boat," T.J. interrupted again. "But I had nothing to do with the plan to bomb it. There's a big difference. You actually believed I was capable of planting explosives as a dramatic protest against the massacre of dolphins by tuna fishermen, Steffie. Maybe your suspicions were fleeting, but the fact is, you were ready to believe I would endanger *human* lives for the sake of saving dolphins." T.J. realized his own temper was flaring despite all the nights he'd spent in self-examination, trying to see Stefanie's point of view, trying to understand why she'd doubted him.

Stefanie closed her eyes and told herself they were going over old ground for no reason. But she knew there was something more she had to say, and she hoped that when she'd said it, she'd be through eating crow. "T.J., I know I was wrong. I knew it almost immediately, though to this day I don't understand where you figured in that incident, especially now that you say you scuttled the boat."

"Can't you figure it out, babe?" T.J. asked, his tone gently persuasive.

"I can't figure out anything! I can't think, I—I can't . . ." Stefanie paused as the whole scene began fitting into place like the parts of a jigsaw puzzle. T.J. had been covering the tuna boat protest in San Francisco. By the time he'd gotten back to New Orleans, she'd seen a picture in a tabloid newspaper that had implicated him in the bombing—though he hadn't been named. She'd recognized her husband, photographed as he'd leapt from the small vessel that had sunk and exploded underwater just moments later.

Suddenly everything took on a new meaning, and Stefanie hated herself even more than during her darkest hours of the past six months. "You scuttled the boat because it was the only way," she said, forcing herself to meet T.J.'s gaze. "Because you'd learned about the bomb and there was no time to dismantle it. Because there were people around who could have been hurt."

She was shocked that she hadn't seen the simple truth before this moment, even though she'd known in every fiber of her being that T.J. wouldn't take part in anything violent, no matter how strongly he advocated direct confrontation—*especially* when he was a journalist covering the event, not a participant. He was too professional. "You might have been killed," she murmured. "And you came home the next day to find that your wife believed, however briefly, that you'd been part of the bomb plot. No wonder you didn't try to explain the truth to me. Under the same circumstances, I wouldn't have bothered either."

"I should have explained," T.J. said, reaching for one of Stefanie's hands and clasping it between his own. "My pride got in the way of a lot of things I should have done at the time, Steffie. I admit I was floored by your reaction. The San Francisco police had accepted my version of the events, but I felt that you'd tried and convicted me without letting me be a witness in my own defense." T.J.'s voice had grown hoarse. "Why, babe? I still don't get it."

Stefanie shook her head. Why? That single word was the question that had been plaguing her without mercy. A photograph in a sleazy tabloid shouldn't make a wife doubt her husband.

She sighed heavily. What was the point of rehashing the whole thing anyway? The marriage was over. She'd dealt it a death blow and didn't even know why. "T.J., let's drop the subject," she said with weary resignation, averting her gaze. "I've admitted I was wrong. I'll still go ahead with the divorce as soon as I get back home. You were right when you accused me of disloyalty, and there's no reason for you to forgive me. There's nothing more I can say or do to make either of us feel better."

T.J. refused to accept Stefanie's defeatist attitude. Somehow he was going to get to the bottom of what really had come between them. He knew his wife was a person of deep, unswerving loyalty to those she loved. He knew she'd loved him. So what had happened to make her lose faith in him for that one crucial moment? "Wrong, babe," he said as he released her hand and motioned to the waiter for the bill. "There's a lot more you can say and do that'll make both of us feel better." Reaching across the table, he crooked his finger under her chin and forced her to look at him. "And you will, darlin'," he told her with quiet determination, then smiled. "I gar-awn-tee it."

The waiter brought the check and T.J. signed for it, then got up and pulled back Stefanie's chair as she rose.

They walked to their rooms in silence. When Stefanie dug out her key from her bag, T.J. automatically took it from her to open the door. To her intense frustration, she realized she'd handed it over just as automatically. Why did she go along with his old-fashioned ways? She was no fragile flower who needed his protection. Yet, reminding herself again that she had to choose her battlegrounds wisely, she said nothing. Still vulnerable to T.J., Stefanie concentrated on resisting any use he chose to make of his considerable charm.

But he surprised her by giving back her key and smiling. "Sweet dreams, babe. I'll see you at breakfast." Then he turned and ambled toward his own door.

Staring after him, Stefanie wasn't sure whether she was relieved, disappointed, or insulted. Didn't he feel the least bit of desire for her? Not that she wanted him to, but his coolness was unsettling.

T.J. reached his door, stopped, and glanced back at Stefanie, remembering his vow to move slowly in reclaiming his wife. During the long nights when he'd relived the events that had destroyed what mattered most to him, he'd decided that the real crux of the problem had been that he and Stefanie had cheated themselves by leaping into marriage without taking time to know each other. After all his blowhard arguments with her about confrontation versus persuasion, why *wouldn't* she have thought the worst of him in a real situation?

Stefanie hadn't let him down any more than he'd let her down, he'd decided months ago.

And now he was trying to start over. He couldn't rush her. It was vital that he take time. A lot of time.

Yet as she stood in front of her door looking at him, her gray eyes filled with conflicting emotions, he felt as if he were hurting her all over again, as if he'd been catapulted back six months to the day when he'd walked out of their apartment.

Not this time, he decided abruptly, pivoting on his heel, striding back to her and unceremoniously hauling her into his arms the way he knew he should have done on that other occasion, the way he would have done if he hadn't been stupidly unyielding.

Caught off guard, Stefanie couldn't utter a single sound of protest as T.J.'s lips descended to hers, his arms closing around her like unbreakable bonds, his tongue aggressively exploring regions he'd once known so well.

The lingering taste of Armagnac suddenly intoxicated Stefanie. Warmth poured into her from T.J.'s body until she melted against him, her arms creeping around his neck, her hands rediscovering the tousled silk of his hair. She felt his rigid, thrusting heat, and instinctively pressed herself against him, a sweet sense of joy rippling through her as she realized he still wanted her. And she wanted him. Dear heaven, how she wanted him. Intense passion drove every sensible thought from her mind, as it had from the very first time T.J. had kissed her. Marriage to any man had been the farthest thing from her mind when she'd met T.J. Carriere. Yet she'd surrendered to him so completely, marriage had seemed inevitable and right.

But it hadn't been right, and here she was, succumbing to him all over again, no lessons learned. The harder she battled the sensations pulsating through her, the more powerful they became. "Johnny," she whispered when T.J. released her mouth and gazed down at her, his eyes dark and searching.

T.J.'s arms tightened around her as he heard the name he'd missed so much. Only Stefanie used the English version of his name—or rather the Scottish, as she'd insisted. Only Stefanie could murmur those two syllables and turn them into a love poem. Only Stefanie could ease the ache that had settled inside him six months before.

With a burst of triumph, he lowered his mouth to hers again, gently this time, yet with undiminished urgency, remembering how Stefanie had loved him to toy with her lips, nibbling, laving with his tongue, savoring her sweetness slowly and thoroughly.

His hunger for her was intensifying at an alarming rate. He cupped one hand behind her head, lacing his fingers through her hair, marveling at its rich texture, recalling how it would brush over his chest like a veil of silk drawn slowly across his skin. Stefanie had known so well how to use those long tresses erotically, sweetly, mysteriously.

For just an instant, the last six months were obliterated. Stefanie was his again, her body melding to his, her lips soft, her hips instinctively moving, driving him wild with need.

Then he remembered: He didn't want those six months obliterated. The time he'd spent away from Stefanie had taught him lessons that would make him a better husband to her. He didn't want to repeat the mistakes of the past, the impulsive decisions based purely on shared passion. Their problems had begun outside the bedroom and had to be resolved outside it. "Baby," he said in a kind of groan as he released her mouth and just held her, trying to regain control of his body, "I didn't mean to do this . . ."

Stefanie twisted out of T.J.'s arms and backed away, staring at him in horror as her sanity returned in a rush. "I didn't mean to do it either," she said, wondering how many times and ways she intended to humiliate herself with this man before she'd had enough. She pulled herself together and spoke as calmly as possible. "Let's try to forget this whole comedy of errors, shall we? After breakfast, we shouldn't need to see each other, so I doubt that anything of this sort will happen again." She pushed open her door and started to step inside.

Grasping her arm, T.J. stopped her in her tracks. He realized she'd misunderstood him, as she'd done so often in the past. "Like I said, darlin', there's no sense running," he told her evenly, deciding simply to throw down the gauntlet and make his position crystal clear. "You may have kept your own name, Stefanie Sinclair, and you may have figured you could return to being the same person you were before you married me. But you have to face the fact that we changed each other the instant we met. Neither of us can go back."

"That's my point exactly," she said in a low voice. "We can't go back."

T.J. reached up to cradle her face between his two hands. "No, we can't. But we can go ahead. We can figure out what went wrong and make sure it doesn't happen again. I don't see you as a quitter, babe. Don't quit on us."

"I'm not the one who quit. You are." Stefanie's control was slipping away rapidly. She was on the verge of breaking down, of giving way to the sobs welling up inside her.

"I thought that was the case for a while myself," T.J. said softly. "But I'm not so certain now."

"Oh, right, T.J., sure. I walked out on you."

"Perhaps, in your own way," he answered. "But why try to place blame? You've heard of no-fault divorce? Why can't we have a no-fault reconciliation? A clean slate?"

Stefanie had to struggle to summon her anger, but she managed at least a decent show. "I'll give you marks for sheer gall, T.J., but if I ever did commit the incredible folly of living with you again, I'd throttle you before a week was out. Your arrogance is mind-boggling!"

T.J. smiled, more bemused than hurt by her words. There was a false ring to Stefanie's anger that he'd heard before. An odd panic. He'd spent months puzzling about the course of several of their quarrels, without gaining much understanding of why they'd happened.

But this time around, he'd promised himself, he would step back and try to figure out what was going on. Drawing on his journalistic background, he would be objective no matter what.

The biggest problem would be her obviously closed mind. But he'd just discovered he had two weapons in his arsenal to breach her wall of defenses: passion and humor. Stefanie could be disarmed, in different ways, by either.

Leaning his forehead against Stefanie's, he grinned, his thumbs stroking her slightly quivering lower lip. "Darlin', you gon' broke mah heart wi' dat talk," he crooned. "Now, you jus' be mah good baby and sleep tight, an' in the mawnin', you'll see. Every li'l thing's gon' be as sweet as crawfish pie." Releasing her, he stolled nonchalantly to his own door, unlocked it, then turned and winked at Stefanie as she stood gaping at him.

In the solitude of his room, he sank to the edge of the bed, his head in his hands, his heart pounding. He was totally exhausted.

Stefanie stood fuming for several more seconds, then went into her room, barely managing not to slam the door, furious with herself for giving T.J. Carriere reason for being so damned cocky.

Three

Despite a fitful night, Stefanie felt strong and in control in the morning.

After she'd showered, dried her hair, and put on her makeup, she'd persuaded herself that T.J. hadn't meant a word of his impulsive reconciliation speech, that he'd reacted sentimentally to the romantic garden wedding, and that he undoubtedly hoped she hadn't taken his words to heart.

The fact that T.J. rarely said things he didn't mean was a detail Stefanie chose to ignore. She also pretended not to feel a flutter in the pit of her stomach as the too-vivid memories of the kisses they'd shared the previous evening nudged at her consciousness.

She dressed quickly in a minimal amount of underwear, a soft, unconstructed taupe jersey jacket and full skirt, a scoop-necked, black silk shell, and low-heeled taupe sandals. The outfit was classic Stefanie Sinclair—comfortable and stylish enough to make her feel equal to any challenge.

Quickly, she packed the last of her things in her tan leather overnight case, left it on the luggage stand, then grabbed her black shoulder bag and strode down to the hotel's café to meet her family for breakfast.

Her aplomb was shaken a little when she saw T.J. looking as gorgeous as ever and chatting amiably with her parents. *One step at a time*, she chanted silently as she smiled and offered a breezy greeting to the gathered clan. Her one regret was that she hadn't been as punctual as usual; the last to arrive, she had to take the only chair available, which was—unsurprisingly—right beside her soon-to-be-ex-husband.

" 'Mornin', babe," he said casually. He wondered if his real feelings showed, if Stefanie had seen the way his heart had skipped a beat when she'd walked into the room. She looked so brisk and businesslike and gorgeous. Her long, tanned, bare legs created havoc with his pulse, her full lips tempted him almost beyond reason. "Did you sleep well?" he asked, surprised at how untroubled he sounded.

"Not especially," she answered, refusing to lie even to save face.

"I guess yesterday's excitement was to blame," he said with a definite ripple of satisfaction in his sea-green eyes.

"I guess it was," she agreed, and picked up the menu, trying not to think about how she'd always loved the clean male scent of him first thing in the morning, when he was freshly shaved and his hair was still damp from the shower. She was annoyed that she actually had to battle an instinctive urge to blurt out how gorgeous he was in his lightweight beige slacks and open-neck shirt, and ivory linen sport jacket.

"To save time, I already ordered your breakfast," he informed her, fully aware that she would consider him presumptuous. But there'd been a time when Stefanie had claimed to appreciate the fact that her husband knew her preferences well enough to order for her in restaurants. T.J. was prepared to court her ire in order to reestablish the rituals that had been part of their life together. "We have a plane to catch," he added innocently.

Stefanie turned to stare at him, hit by a double whammy. The fact that he'd ordered for her was maddening, but his last statement was alarming. "What do you mean?" she asked, her expression wary.

"I told the waitress to bring your favorites: orange juice, hotcakes, and blueberry syrup . . ."

"That's not what I'm talking about," she said through clenched teeth. "What was that comment about how *we* have a plane to catch? Are you saying you're taking the same flight to Miami as I am?"

"And the one from Miami to New Orleans," T.J. answered cheerfully. He glanced past Stefanie at the approaching waitress. "Here comes breakfast, and not a minute too soon. I don't know about everybody else, but I'm starved."

Stefanie spoke in a low voice as the food was being served and her sisters and parents were conversing among themselves. "Did Morgan arrange his-and-hers plane tickets too?"

"No, darlin', I'm responsible for those arrangements, though I admit I did ask Morgan about your travel plans."

"So you're following me."

"Honey, I'm just going back to my hometown, same as you are. Don't I have the right? I thought it would be nice if we traveled together. Don't you?"

"It won't work," Stefanie said, attacking her hotcakes with purpose. "I'm going to call a lawyer tomorrow, and that's that."

T.J. noticed that an awkward silence had fallen over the table, so he dug into his bacon and eggs and smiled at Stefanie's parents. "You know, one of the things I've always admired about your daughters is the way they appreciate food. It says something about them and about the way they were raised. Good, healthy, uninhibited appetites are so appealing in a female. Don't you agree, Charlie?"

Though Stefanie's father's lips twitched in a small grin that reminded T.J. of Stefanie when she was trying not to laugh, Charlie gave his head a little shake as if warning T.J. not to go too far unless he wanted a pitcher of blueberry syrup dumped over his head.

Inclined to heed the older, wiser man's silent advice, T.J. turned his attention to Lisa and Heather. "How are the European branches of Dreamweavers, Inc. coming along?"

Heather's huge, expressive eyes, which dominated her heart-shaped face and were framed by wayward curls, suddenly lit up, revealing how excited she was about her work. "The British division is doing great," she said enthusiastically. "It's amazing how many people are fascinated by medieval castles, ghost stories, and unsolved mysteries and such. Our London office can't keep up with the demand, and we're going crazy in Edinburgh just months after start-up."

T.J. turned to Stefanie. "Well, babe, as president of Dreamweavers, you must be glad you encouraged your baby sister to go ahead with her haunted-house tours. It took a lot of faith to trust a twenty-two-year-old to pull off the idea."

Stefanie swallowed a syrup-drenched bit of hotcake, took a sip of coffee, gave T.J. a phony smile, then beamed a more genuine grin at Heather. "Her operation is a little more complex than haunted-house tours, but, yes. We're all proud of the way Heather showed us she had the right idea at the right time."

"So did Lisa," Heather put in loyally. "And Morgan, and you, Steffie." With youthful excitement, Heather tried to bring T.J. up to date in a single torrent of words. "Steffie's Mississippi riverboat cruises are going like gangbusters, Morgan's about to add a third pirate ship to her line, and Lisa's cultural tours are being raved about in European travel circles as the 'in' thing to do. One magazine critic touted her Provence Pilgrimage as practically essential to any art student's education, and—"

Laughing, Lisa put her hand on her younger sister's arm. "Heather, I love hearing you brag about me, but why don't we modestly agree that we're all fabulous successes and leave it at that?"

T.J. chuckled at Lisa's quiet, understated humor, realizing anew how much he loved this family, how deeply he'd missed being part of it. With Lisa living in southern France, Heather in Scotland, Morgan in Key West, and Stefanie in New Orleans, the four sisters got together only occasionally, but distance hadn't lessened their closeness a bit. Unbreakable bonds had been forged among them when they'd grown up on the family's sailing vessel, the *Dreamweaver.*

Their parents still roamed the world on that same boat, stopping for periodic sojourns to gather research for their widely read anthropology books, so it was a rare treat when the entire group gathered at one time. T.J. hated to see the breakfast end despite his eagerness to be alone again with Stefanie.

But it did end, and T.J. found himself getting nervous. His bravado was a tough act to keep up.

Stefanie knew there was no way to avoid traveling with T.J., short of being childish enough to change her ticket—which wouldn't help anyway, because he could change his too. She simply didn't understand why he was being so stubborn all of a sudden, claiming to want a reconciliation. Why would he? Especially, she thought with a shaft of unhappiness she didn't want to recognize, since T.J. hadn't said a word about still loving her.

She finished her coffee and turned to her mother. "Mom, will you come back to my room while I freshen up and get my bag?"

"Of course, dear." After letting Stefanie go ahead a little, Kate got up, smiled sweetly at T.J., and bent to whisper to him, "I believe I'm about to answer for our family's intrigues on your behalf, young man. If you win your reconciliation with Stefanie, don't ever give us reason to be sorry we helped."

T.J. stared after the woman as she followed Stefanie. He finally understood exactly what was meant by an iron hand in a velvet glove. Kate Sinclair was petite, almost fragile looking, her hair a soft, silvery blond, her voice gentle. But she had as much sheer presence as any of her daughters and had kept her giant of a husband enchanted and slightly mystified for some thirty-three years.

"You heard Mom," Lisa said when Stefanie and Kate were out of earshot. "We're helping you on sheer faith, T.J., because we haven't the faintest idea what went wrong between you two. Stefanie isn't talking."

T.J. frowned, surprised that Stefanie hadn't confided in her family. "I'm not sure myself what went wrong," he admitted. "So I can't make any promises about the future, except that I'll never hurt Stefanie in any way if I can help it."

Charlie cleared his throat. "Any man who promises more is either insincere or unrealistic, son. I just hope you know what kind of challenge you've taken on with my daughter. She can be one muleheaded, high-spirited little filly, that one."

Lisa and Heather stared at their father. "Muleheaded?" Lisa repeated.

"Filly?" Heather said.

Charlie laughed. "Your mother and I have decided to do our next book on a really exotic culture: American cowboys trying to keep their identity while adapting to a high-tech world. I guess the background reading is creeping into my vocabulary."

"Maybe so," T.J. said, grinning at his father-in-law. "But that particular description of Stefanie is right on the mark. In fact, I'd do well to study the techniques of a bronco-busting rodeo cowboy. They might come in handy."

Heather giggled. "T.J. Carriere, the Cajun Cowboy," she said, adding with a dreamy sigh, "Gosh, doesn't it sound romantic?"

Lisa groaned and shook her head. "There she goes again. Heather Sinclair, one of these days you're going to wake up like Sleeping Beauty, only you'll see cold reality staring you in the face, not Prince Charming."

Heather merely laughed, but Charlie and T.J. exchanged a sharp glance. Perhaps Stefanie wasn't the only Sinclair woman who wasn't confiding in the others about problems in her love life, T.J. thought. There had been a distinct and uncharacteristic edge in Lisa's voice.

He sighed inwardly. Was Lisa right? Was he like Heather, living in a dream world where every story had a happy ending? Would he soon wake up to find cold reality staring *him* in the face, instead of Stefanie's luminous eyes?

Not if he could help it, he told himself with renewed resolution.

"Why, Mom?" Stefanie said as soon as she and her mother were in the privacy of her room. "Why is my whole family siding with T.J. and ganging up on me? You could have booked the same flight I did, but instead you claimed you wanted to stick around and see more of the Keys. I don't believe that excuse anymore. I don't buy the story Heather and Lisa gave me about the flight being full either. You're trying to force me to be alone with T.J., and it isn't fair!" She plopped down on the edge of the bed as if to punctuate her complaint.

Kate lowered herself to a chair and smiled with genuine sympathy. "Why are you so afraid to be alone with T.J., dear?"

Stefanie closed her eyes and spoke slowly, unable to be less than honest with her mother. "Because I'm attracted to him," she admitted. "And he knows it. He says he wants me back, but . . ." Her voice trailed off as a huge lump formed in her throat.

"What's the problem between you two?" Kate asked gently. "What happened to tear you apart?"

Stefanie got up and paced back and forth beside

the bed. "We got married, that's what happened. I still can't believe I stood up in front of a justice of the peace and pledged my whole life to a man I'd known for three weeks. It just wasn't *me* to do such a thing! And I don't even have the excuse of youth, because I was almost thirty years old when I married T.J. Carriere. I guess I have to plead temporary insanity. It's the only explanation. I'm not right for T.J., Mom. He needs some sweet, self-effacing lady who's soft and compliant, not an opinionated creature used to running her own life. At the very least, he should find someone who's even-tempered. Perhaps if I were more like Morgan—"

"Then you wouldn't be Stefanie, which would be a dreadful loss."

Stefanie turned and grinned. "Spoken like a true mother. You're not exactly objective about all this, you know."

"I should hope not. But tell me what really frightens you about your husband."

"He's not my husband, and he doesn't frighten me."

"He *is* your husband, and he terrifies you. Why?"

Stefanie began pacing again. "Okay, all right, let's say he—he bugs me. He calls me *baby*, did you know that? Me. *Baby*. It's laughable."

"Well now, that's certainly grounds for divorce," Kate said, clucking her tongue. "I had no idea the man was so abusive."

"Moth-ther!" Stefanie said in total frustration, then sat on the bed and buried her face in her hands, realizing she sounded like a bratty adolescent. Raising her head a moment later, she took a deep breath and tried to explain. "It's not the word. It's the attitude behind the word. It's T.J.'s entire outlook. He's from another century. He wants a woman he can pet and spoil and—and own. Fine. That's his problem. I just don't want it to be mine."

Kate moved from her chair to sit beside Stefanie on the end of the bed, putting her arm around her daughter's shoulders. "Are you sure it isn't already your problem?"

Stefanie gave her mother a guarded look. "Uh-oh. This is what I get for having a sociologist as my mother. Okay, Mom. Hit me with it. Exactly what are you suggesting?"

Kate shook her head and chuckled quietly, giving her daughter a quick hug. "Just that your father and I pursued an unusual way of life, what with moving around so much and living a lot of the time on our boat. You never had much chance to be a baby. You were aware of problems and dangers when your sisters were too young to understand things such as money being short or storms threatening to swamp us—you were responsible and mature far beyond your years, taking care of the other kids, protecting them, riding herd on them when you thought it was necessary. I feel a bit guilty about you, Stefanie. You've spent a lot of time looking after other people, but no one ever looked after you, until T.J. came along."

Stefanie wasn't sure she liked the direction of her mother's thoughts. "So what's your point, Mom?"

"Don't you find it significant that the first man you really responded to was one who was prepared to do for you what you've always done for others? That you were nearly thirty before you lapsed into temporary insanity or, as most of us call it, fell in love? That the only man who can make your knees turn to jelly is the one who has never let you ride herd on him?"

Stefanie definitely didn't like what her mother was suggesting. She jumped to her feet. "Well, I'm wrong to respond to that kind of man, and my knees are wrong to turn to jelly. And if I don't hurry up, I'll miss my plane and T.J. will scold me for being a naughty little girl."

Kate laughed. "You'll never make me believe T.J. tries to baby you in that sense. He has too much respect for you to be patronizing."

"Ha!" Stefanie retorted, picking up her overnight bag and slinging the strap over her shoulder, at the same time yanking open the door and holding it for her mother.

Kate stood and kissed Stefanie's cheek. "You always were the one with the snappy comebacks," she said with a mischievous wink.

The flight to Miami was every bit as excruciating as Stefanie had feared it would be. For the second day in a row, she found herself seated next to T.J., her shoulder and arm pressed against his, her senses responding to his touch and fragrance and the sound of his voice.

As the plane taxied down the runway, T.J. took Stefanie's hand in his and grinned at her, and she remembered admitting to him in a foolishly trusting moment that an aircraft's takeoff always gave her a thrill that was oddly sensual.

It was difficult to fight a man who knew her so intimately, she thought, leaning her head against the backrest and closing her eyes, hating herself for responding exactly as T.J. had known she would.

She hated herself, too, for the feelings that intensified because he was aware of them, because his fingers tightened around hers as the plane lifted off, because the warmth of him was coursing through her.

She wondered how he could understand her so well, when they'd been together such a short time. She'd met all sorts of long-married couples who had no idea of each other's secret thoughts and feelings. Admittedly, she'd found it easy to be open with T.J., to confide in him. He was an attentive, understanding listener. It was one of his many charms.

All at once, Stefanie wondered why on earth she *was* fighting him. Despite the arguments, the constant clashes of will, she'd never been as happy as when she'd been with T.J., never as alive, as filled with exhilaration. Being with him again could be so sweet, she thought. He had carried her to heights greater than any airplane could fly.

T.J. didn't release her hand when they'd reached cruising altitude, and Stefanie couldn't seem to summon the will to wrest herself free.

With her eyes still closed, she heard the flight attendant's offer of refreshments, then T.J.'s quiet, polite refusal. He'd made another decision for her, Stefanie thought wearily. But she couldn't complain. As usual, it was the right decision. T.J. knew she wouldn't want anything so soon after breakfast.

Turning her head, she opened her eyes and saw that he, too, was resting, his eyes shut, his head tilted back. Perhaps he hadn't slept any better the night before than she had.

Instead of looking away, as she knew she should, Stefanie gave in to the temptation to study T.J.'s profile, mentally tracing the strong line of his jaw, the curve of his sensual lips, the slight arch of his brows. With a half smile, she remembered how she'd teased him about his ridiculously thick, long lashes and naturally wavy hair.

Suddenly she realized she'd been caught: T.J. turned to look at her, and as Stefanie gazed into his green eyes, she felt as if she were being drawn into the vortex of a looking-glass world filled with mystery and enchantment.

"Hi, babe," T.J. said softly.

Stefanie watched, hypnotized, as he brought her hand to his lips and kissed the backs of her fingers. "T.J., you can't want me back," she protested lamely. "We fought so much."

"I know, darlin'," he answered, shaken by Stefanie's soft expression. "But we didn't give ourselves time to learn to compromise—not before the wedding and not afterward. All I ask is that we go back to the beginning and try doing things the right way. I think we always needed a proper courtship, babe. The old-fashioned kind. Won't you give us a chance to have it?"

Stefanie's fragile resistance began crumbling. T.J. was so persuasive, and she did care so deeply for him. Yet those very feelings were part of the problem: The pain of losing T.J. a second time would be too much to bear, and she was almost certain that the loss was inevitable. Despite the delicious making-up sessions that had followed their quarrels, any battle could escalate out of control the way their last one had. She didn't want a repeat of that kind of scene.

T.J. would have given a great deal to know what was going through Stefanie's mind. He could sense her mental wheels turning and knew she was mulling over his suggestion. But whether her thoughts were for or against him, he couldn't guess. Reaching up with his free hand to lay his palm over her cheek, he gently drew her head down to his shoulder. When she didn't resist, he pressed his lips to the top of her head, trying not to let his momentary happiness blind him to the all-too-real difficulties that still lay ahead.

But maybe, just maybe, he was going to get his wife back after all.

Four

Stefanie's lips were pressed together and her skin was ashen as the plane began its descent to Miami in the midst of a violent storm.

Aware that she wouldn't admit to being even a trifle nervous, T.J. merely held her hand and chatted idly, pretending not to notice the tightening of her fingers around his, the shadow of fear in her eyes.

He wasn't surprised that she remained tense after they'd touched down and taxied to the terminal; Stefanie was bothered by the storm itself, not by flying through it.

The airport was a scene of utter pandemonium as outgoing flights were cancelled and scheduled arrivals were rerouted due to hurricane warnings in the Miami area.

"What kind of wait are we facing?" Stefanie asked as T.J. returned from the ticket counter where he'd checked on the status of their flight to New Orleans.

"At least overnight," T.J. answered, not at all

upset about the delay. He was in no hurry to get back to New Orleans if staying in Miami meant he could have Stefanie to himself a little longer. "I'd suggest we both start phoning around for a hotel room."

"Hotel rooms," Stefanie amended in a strained voice that betrayed her raw nerves. She tried to smile. "As in two separate ones."

T.J. shrugged. "Whatever you say, darlin', but from what I understand, we'll be lucky to find anything in this town tonight. Apparently the city is booked solid with conventions, and now, with all these stranded people . . ."

Glancing toward a bank of phones where she saw people repeatedly punching out numbers and shaking their heads, Stefanie said, "I see what you mean. Let's start by getting out of this crush and grabbing a taxi to the nearest shopping mall so I can use a phone without waiting in another long lineup. I have friends in Miami. I'm sure one of them would put us up."

T.J. put his hand on the small of Stefanie's back to steer her through the crowd toward the exit. "Is there any major city where you don't have friends?" he asked, adding with a grin, "I'd almost forgotten about the network you've built up over the years. It surely does smooth out life's little wrinkles, babe. No wonder I can't get along without you."

T.J.'s gentle teasing had its usual effect. It lifted Stefanie's mood and made her smile despite her edginess. "Last night you said you wanted me back to nurse you in your old age, and today you suggest my irresistible attractiveness lies in my contacts. You'll turn my head with these extravagant compliments, Johnny."

He laughed, pleased by her use of the special nickname.

Outside, Stefanie groaned at the chaos. "What was it I said about grabbing a taxi? What made me think it would be that easy? This is a madhouse!"

"Trust me, babe," T.J. said nonchalantly.

Moments later, settled into the back seat of a taxi, Stefanie smiled again at T.J. "You know, I have to admit it again: There are moments when your aggressive tendencies come in handy."

T.J. smiled, deeply pleased by Stefanie's increasing willingness to accept him as he was, "aggressive tendencies" and all. He also seized the opportunity to slip in a remark in support of his cause. "So we're a good team, right?"

Stefanie couldn't help agreeing with him on that score. In countless ways, they always had been a good team. Their only problem was that both of them instinctively expected to be captain.

They reached a mall and found a phone. Within five minutes Stefanie was giving T.J. a nod as she hung up. "We're all set. A friend of mine has an extra bedroom and a couch."

Though T.J. was relieved to have a place to put their heads for the night, he couldn't help wishing they would be sharing a pillow.

"I'd like to phone my office," she said, already punching out the number.

"On Sunday?" T.J. asked.

"My secretary said she'd be in for a while to do some catch-up work."

As T.J. waited, he noticed Stefanie frowning then talking animatedly. "Any problems?" he asked when she'd finished the call.

"Nothing major. My nemesis is on the warpath,

that's all. Stuart Gardner—of Gardner Chemicals—stormed into my office on Friday demanding to see me, furious about the media hassle and bureaucratic heat he's taking at last."

"I'm not sure I like the sound of things," T.J. said as he and Stefanie went outside to find another cab. "The man went to your office to see you? Isn't he being a little extreme?"

Stefanie nodded. "But at least we're getting to the man if he's dropped his mask of disdain long enough to come to talk to me."

"Why you, Steffie? As I recall, there are a number of other well-known, highly vocal activists in your environmental group."

"Who knows?" Stefanie answered, not quite truthfully. Recalling all too well how livid T.J. could be if he thought she was being insulted or threatened in any way—and how he tended to forget she was capable of fighting her own battles—she chose not to mention that Gardner had picked on her because he thought she had a chink in her armor that he could use to scare her off. What Gardner didn't know, Stefanie thought, her anger simmering just below the boiling point as she bristled at the way he'd bullied her secretary, was that Stefanie Sinclair didn't scare easily. "There's a cab, T.J.," she said briskly.

"I see it," T.J. answered, raising his hand. What he also saw was that Stefanie was keeping something from him. The knowledge was slightly depressing. If she had some kind of problem, he wanted to help. But, as usual, Stefanie didn't want him involved in her concerns. She didn't trust him.

Despite his disappointment in Stefanie's unwillingness to confide in him, T.J. had to smile at the efficient way she gave the driver the address plus explicit directions for reaching their destination. Stefanie wouldn't let the cabbie choose the route if she could help it, T.J. thought with amused affection, enjoying her instinctive air of authority.

Only when she became compulsive about her need to be on top of things and in control did he find himself driven to distraction—partly, he had admitted to himself during one especially long night filled with self-recrimination, because he was something of a controller himself. But living without Stefanie had taught him a hard lesson about priorities. He was prepared to learn to make concessions and compromises.

The huge, unknown factor in his reconciliation bid was whether Stefanie would meet him halfway. Not even halfway, he thought. A quarter of the way would do. He was like an old-time vacuum cleaner salesman: All he needed was to get his foot in the door.

He wondered if the bonus of an overnight delay would give him a chance to be alone with Stefanie. Perhaps her friend would have a date for the evening or would go to bed early. It was something to hope for, he told himself.

When they reached the address, T.J. paid the driver while Stefanie went into the apartment building's foyer to buzz her friend.

It occurred to Stefanie, as she and T.J. went inside and stepped into the elevator, that she was being a little unfair to him, but she rationalized her lie of omission. She'd been distracted by the news of Gardner's visit. And, remembering T.J.'s moments of jealousy, she'd decided that seeing his reaction to her friend could be enlightening. At a time when she was tempted to think she couldn't live without

T.J., she could use a reminder of one of the reasons why she couldn't live *with* the man. She knocked on the apartment door without giving him the slightest warning of what was in store. The door opened.

So did T.J.'s mouth.

"Mom!" their host said in a deep baritone, throwing his arms around Stefanie and giving her a bear hug that lifted her right off her feet.

T.J. swallowed hard, realizing he should have suspected something when Stefanie hadn't offered any details about her friend. He couldn't help wondering whether she'd kept quiet on purpose. Was she testing to see whether he was still as possessive as ever?

Unfortunately, he was. He had a long way to go before he'd conquer his jealous impulses, judging by his sudden urge to pry Stefanie and her muscle-bound pal apart and slug the guy. And what was this *Mom* business?

Deciding that the embrace had gone on long enough, T.J. loudly cleared his throat.

Stefanie turned to him as if just remembering he was there. "Oh, T.J., I guess you haven't met Brad Packard. You must remember my mentioning him."

"It's great to meet you," Brad said, releasing Stefanie to pump T.J.'s hand enthusiastically.

T.J. smiled absently, searching his memory, certain he'd have recalled any mention Stefanie might have made about this bronzed, sun-streaked, centerfold-handsome male.

"Come on inside," Brad said jovially, taking both Stefanie's and T.J.'s bags. He winked at Stefanie. "T.J. looks a mite confused, Mom."

"Brad was my college roommate," she explained to T.J., barely suppressing a giggle.

Recollections began clicking into place in T.J.'s

mind, like photographic slides in a fast-moving projector. But the images coming into sharp focus gave him a shock. He'd conjured up a very different Brad Packard from the one he was looking at. A jock, Stefanie had said. A fullback. So why hadn't the man's nose been flattened a few times? Why did he have all his teeth? Why wasn't he walking on his knuckles?

T.J.'s eyes narrowed as he returned his gaze to Stefanie. He wasn't certain she'd created this unflattering mind picture deliberately, but she definitely hadn't offered all the details. He made himself return her smile as it occurred to him he was being baited. "You mean Brad was one of several roommates, don't you, babe? In that big house a bunch of you rented?"

"That's right," Stefanie said, wondering whether T.J. was as cool as he appeared. He could be building up to an eruption, she realized, wondering if she'd been wise to test him this way.

But T.J. smiled pleasantly. "It took me a minute to put things together, Brad. Stefanie has told me about you, but she left out a few things." He paused and fixed her with a level gaze, letting his words sink in, then turned back to Brad with a look of amusement. "My wife never mentioned that you think she's your mother for instance."

"We all thought she was our mother," Brad said, laughing heartily as he put T.J.'s bag in the entryway closet.

"Because she's so maternal?" T.J. asked.

Brad hooted. "Because she's so bossy!" He put his arm around Stefanie to give her a quick hug. "But she's lovable anyway."

"I know what you mean," T.J. said through slightly

clenched teeth. He glanced around the luxurious apartment, taking in the leather sofa and marble-and-smoked-glass tables. The furnishings all but shouted that Brad was a major success. "It's good of you to put us up," he murmured politely.

"I'm more than glad to have you," Brad answered, heading toward the apartment's bedrooms. "Make yourselves comfortable while I put Mom's bag in the spare room." He disappeared, leaving Stefanie and T.J. alone for a moment.

"Nice guy," T.J. said in a clipped tone, moving through the room as if extremely interested in the ultracontemporary decor.

"Brad is a dear." Stefanie eyed T.J. warily. He was being awfully calm, she thought. It just didn't ring true. Obviously, T.J. knew she'd expected him to be furious that Brad was much more attractive than she'd let on in the past. All this calm acceptance had to be an act.

Aware of Stefanie's gaze following him, T.J. was dead certain she was waiting for him to revert to form. He refused to live down to her expectations. "So you and Brad have maintained your friendship all these years?" he asked with seemingly detached interest, lowering himself to the couch and glancing through a coffee table book that he quickly realized was filled with erotic art prints.

"Of course," Stefanie said with a hint of triumph in her voice, sure she'd heard an accusation in T.J.'s voice. "And isn't it a good thing Brad and I have stayed close? He's being a real lifesaver for us tonight."

T.J. stopped turning pages to study one print in particular, deliberately exaggerating his interest in it.

Stefanie walked over to stand near enough to see what had caught his attention, but he quickly turned the page. Even so, the picture Stefanie had caught a glimpse of made her gasp. "Good grief, T.J., close that book!"

He looked up with a surprised smile. "Why? I'm sure Brad has seen these pictures." Peering even more intently at the print, T.J. gave his head a little shake. "And you and I have acted out a few of them, as I recall." T.J. was playing it cool with a supreme effort of will. He didn't care for the idea that Stefanie had lived with a man who kept erotic art on his coffee table. "You did say you and Brad had a purely platonic relationship?" he couldn't resist asking.

"Purely," Stefanie said, lifting her chin, deciding that T.J. was about to show his true colors. "And if you embarrass me when Brad comes back by—" She stopped abruptly as Brad returned.

"You mentioned you hadn't eaten lunch," Brad said, beaming a dazzling smile at Stefanie. "I've put together some pasta with my famous sauce bolognese. And I've whipped up your favorite dressing for the salad, Mom."

T.J. started using Stefanie's self-control trick of mentally listing the vice presidents. He would *not* react. Not if it killed him to be pleasant.

"I'll give you a hand in the kitchen, Brad," Stefanie suggested, suddenly not sure she wanted to be alone with T.J.

T.J. cut off his list at Martin Van Buren and got to his feet. "I have a better idea, babe. You sit here and let the men do the work. I want to get acquainted with Brad, and let's face it, what better place is there for a couple of guys to get down to the nitty-gritty than a kitchen?"

Stefanie sank to the couch, realizing that T.J. had outmaneuvered her. If she objected, he might suggest she didn't want him to be alone with Brad because she had something to hide. "Come to think of it," she said with a tight smile, "I rather like the idea of being waited on by a couple of men."

T.J. moved toward her and gave her a peck on the cheek. "I thought you might, babe."

Brad chuckled and led T.J. to the kitchen.

Absently, Stefanie began thumbing through the book on the coffee table.

T.J. poked his head back into the room. "Page fifty-seven, darlin'."

Stefanie slammed the book shut and got up. She moved restlessly around the room, finally stopping at the window to stare out at the ugly black clouds blanketing the sky. She dreaded the growing fury of the storm.

Yet, despite her deep-seated fears, she found herself smiling, forced to concede that sparring with T.J. was the most fun she'd had in a long time.

"So finally I get to meet the man our level-headed, practical Steffie eloped with," Brad remarked when he had set out the salad ingredients. "It seems funny to think of Mom with a husband. Or an ex-husband, I guess."

"Husband," T.J. said pleasantly.

"But separated?"

"For now."

Brad smiled. "I take it you want a reconciliation."

T.J. began tearing lettuce leaves. "You take it right."

"Can't say I blame you," Brad said as he cut a

tomato into segments. "That lady can be pretty stubborn, though."

"I guess you'd know," T.J. said.

"I sure do." Brad set the tomato aside and peeled a Bermuda onion. "And no, T.J., we were never more than roommates."

T.J. looked up in surprise. "Am I that obvious?"

"You're doing pretty well, considering the circumstances."

"Why weren't you more than roommates?" T.J. asked, trying in vain not to sound too contrary.

"I don't know," Brad said with a careless shrug of his wide shoulders. "I guess Steffie's not my type, and I got the message early that I wasn't hers. She has a way of sending out not-interested signals even when she's being friendly."

"Signals?" T.J. said, puzzled. "What kinds of signals?"

"You probably wouldn't recognize them. She's different with you. Her whole attitude toward you is . . . I don't know. Different, that's all." Brad paused, then forged ahead. "There's an obvious chemistry between you two. A definite sizzle of excitement. What I can't figure is why you and Steffie broke up."

T.J. was pleased by Brad's words. It hadn't occurred to him that Stefanie's powerful sensuality was directed only at him, that other men received entirely different messages from her. "Why did we break up?" he asked, beginning to warm to Brad. "That's a question I've asked myself constantly for the past six months. I have to admit we fought a lot. I'm no angel to live with, and I believe you've noticed that Stefanie has a . . . shall we say . . . a dynamic personality?"

Brad threw back his head and laughed. "Nicely

put. Steffie's not a domineering woman, though. She can be pig-headed—"

"Maybe obstinate," T.J. said quietly, rankling a bit at the choice of words.

Brad laughed again. "Obstinate, then. Sorry. Steffie once said you were pretty protective. I see what she means. Anyway, when she's being obstinate, it's only because she's convinced she's right—and most of the time she is. She's a bright lady, in case you haven't noticed. And she's smart enough not to fall for some wimp she could push around, so you should be glad you two fight. In your case, I'd say a little battling is healthy." Brad reached into a high cupboard as T.J. rinsed the lettuce leaves. "By the way, you'd better use this salad spinner. Steffie gave it to me because she said I never dried the greens properly."

T.J. grinned, put in the lettuce, and gave it a few good whirls. "What do you think?" he asked as he lifted the lid of the spinner. "Will Stefanie be satisfied?"

Brad didn't bother looking. "It's entirely up to you, T.J., but you've got my vote of confidence."

Before another hour had passed, T.J. knew his hopes for an evening alone with Stefanie were doomed. The storm was reaching near-hurricane intensity, and Brad couldn't be expected to go out in it even if he felt like playing Cupid.

Besides, Brad and Stefanie had a lot of old times to reminisce about, gossip to catch up on. T.J. found himself enjoying the evening, content to watch Stefanie as she curled up in a chair and chatted with Brad, exchanging funny anecdotes and jokes, and inevitably indulging her habit of making silly wagers on everything from trivia questions to the amount of time that would pass between two bursts of thunder.

T.J. knew that a large part of Stefanie's gaiety was bravado as the storm worsened. If he hadn't known her so well, he'd never have guessed at the turmoil inside her. Brad didn't seem to notice.

Even when the storm knocked out the lights, Stefanie's only outward reaction was to become quiet, her manner unnaturally subdued, though Brad quickly brought out candles and hurricane lamps.

T.J. ached to enfold Stefanie in his arms and simply hold her. But he knew she wouldn't allow herself to cling to him for comfort, even if Brad weren't around. Stefanie hated to show any kind of weakness. They had been married for two months when a storm in the middle of the night woke her from a deep sleep. T.J. had seen the stark terror in her eyes, and it had haunted him ever since.

She wouldn't talk about her feelings, wouldn't even admit having them. A stupid nightmare, she'd called her lapse on that one occasion, laughing it off.

Trying to understand his wife, T.J. had spoken to Stefanie's parents about the incident.

"Steffie was only eight when we were cruising in the South Pacific and a minor typhoon blew up," her father had explained. "We'd anchored in a sheltered, safe cove, but some of the extra ropes mooring us to shore came loose during the night. Kate and I went out to secure them again, so Stefanie was left below to take care of her little sisters. Morgan was five, Lisa three, and Heather a year old."

"It was a hair-raising night," Charlie had admitted. "But mostly for Stefanie. She didn't realize her mother and I had things under control, yet even in the midst of her conviction that we were all doomed, she tried to give her sisters confidence. Steffie gathered the three little ones onto her bed, sitting cross-legged with her back wedged against the wall, Heather tucked into her lap, Lisa and Morgan wrapped in her arms."

Charlie had paused, shaking his head as he recalled the scene he and his wife had found when they'd returned to the children after about an hour. "It was all we could do to pry the little ones loose from Stefanie's fierce hold," he'd said in a subdued tone. "I'll never forget that little girl's white-lipped expression, the look in her eyes. Yet she wouldn't admit she'd been frightened, not then or later. Morgan told us that Steffie spent the whole time saying that the tossing and turning was fun, that it was like a circus ride. Morgan, of course, had the time of her life, giggling and wanting more. But for Stefanie, it was an awful ordeal."

T.J. wondered how many storms Stefanie had endured alone in the past six months.

With a secret wink at T.J., Brad suddenly stood, stretched, and yawned. "I'm beat, folks. Would you think I was a lousy host if I went to bed?"

"Not at all," T.J. said with a little too much enthusiasm.

"Of course not," Stefanie murmured, though she was alarmed at the prospect of being alone with T.J.

Brad put out linens for T.J. to use on the couch, offered a good night that Stefanie found maddeningly cheerful, then abandoned her, leaving her to choose between staying with T.J. and going to bed while the storm was raging outside.

She didn't want T.J. to know how nervous he made her, so she remained curled up in her chair as if she hadn't a care in the world. "Brad's such a great guy," she said, unable to think of anything else to talk about.

"He is," T.J. agreed, adding, "I still find it hard to figure how you two could have lived together without getting involved." He was no longer jealous of Brad; he was merely curious.

"And you don't believe it, I suppose," Stefanie said defensively, deciding that T.J.'s mask was about to slip away. "I'm sure you can't imagine that two people of the opposite sex could sleep in the same house without deciding to gravitate toward the same bed."

"Hey, babe, don't start putting words into my mouth. I believe you. I was asking, that's all."

Her nagging conscience whispered to Stefanie that she was trying to stir up trouble, determined to take T.J.'s comment the wrong way, but she barreled ahead. "You believe me? How nice. Of course, since I hadn't met you at the time, it's really no concern of yours what I did or didn't do with Brad, is it? But then, we both know you'd like your wife to have lived in a cloister until you came along."

"Stefanie, don't you see what you're doing?" T.J. said, scowling as he watched her try to start a fight all by herself.

"In the vernacular, I'm telling it like it is," she said, getting to her feet. "I'm calling it as I see it. You acted admirably all evening with Brad, but it was a performance. You're as possessive as ever. You want some whey-faced little mouse who's never had a thought or a life of her own, and I don't fill the bill . . ." Her words trailed off as she suddenly had to swallow hard, her mouth dry. She was stunned to recognize the sheer panic in her voice, the utter nonsense of what she was saying.

T.J. stood, walked over to her, and dragged her into his arms.

Stefanie was paralyzed with shock, but she tried

to protest. "T.J., why don't you hate me? I'm impossible! You can't want to put up with all my—"

"Shh," he interrupted, looking down at her with a tender smile. "I finally get it, babe. You're running scared. Not just about being alone with me tonight—I expected that reaction. But this little tirade has opened my eyes. You started running scared the day we were married and you realized you had let me get too close. You'd lost some of the autonomy you were used to having. So you panicked and started tail-spinning into instigating these phony quarrels, trying to push me away to a safe distance." He bent to touch his mouth to hers briefly, then he spoke softly, persuasively. "It's not going to work, Stefanie. I see through you at long last. I won't be pushed away."

"I have no idea what you're talking about," Stefanie protested in a small voice, shaken by the possibility that T.J. had cut straight through her smoke screen to the truth. "What on earth are you going on about?"

"You're smart enough to figure it out," he said, recapturing her mouth, his lips moving gently over hers, gradually increasing their demands until her resistance began dissolving, her body softening, her tongue meeting his, her arms winding around his neck.

Stefanie lost all sense of time or place as T.J.'s warmth flowed into her, his strong arms offering a haven she craved, his kisses driving out her fears. Yet, when he released her mouth for just a moment, she still tried to resist the languor creeping over her. "Johnny, I don't want to let you affect me this way," she whispered.

"You don't have any choice," he answered softly. "And neither do I." Then he crushed her mouth under his without mercy, his hand moving down to caress Stefanie's throat and the upper slope of her breast, finally cupping one firm mound. He felt as if he would explode when her nipple hardened and thrust into his palm through her clothes. Memories flooded back to drive him wild: Stefanie's lithe, golden body responding eagerly to his every touch; Stefanie's long legs wrapping around his hips; Stefanie gazing up at him, moving in a perfect rhythm with his deep thrusts, arching herself to receive everything he could give her.

"Johnny," she kept whispering as T.J.'s kisses burned her throat and earlobe. "Johnny, I want you so much. I can't help it, Johnny. Whatever else is between us, I can't stop wanting you . . ."

"Not here," he said with a low groan. He needed Stefanie more than he'd ever dreamed possible, but he didn't want their first union after so long a separation to be hampered by the presence of a third person. And they were repeating their past mistakes, he realized. They were going too fast. "Not here, baby. Not with Brad in the other room."

Stefanie was plunged back into the real world with an unpleasant start. T.J. was right. For a moment, she'd forgotten Brad. But she was hurt and embarrassed that she'd asked T.J. to make love to her, and he'd turned her down.

Twisting out of his arms, she took a deep breath to regain control as she stepped away from him. "That was rotten, T.J. Carriere. Just plain rotten. What were you doing, simply proving you could get to me? Well, you don't have to prove it. You can. Are you happy now? Has your ego been fed enough?" A crack of lightning made Stefanie jump, made her heart pound even more wildly. "I'm going to bed," she muttered, making a wide circle around T.J. as she hurried past him toward her room.

" 'Night, babe," T.J. said quietly, refusing to defend himself. He didn't blame Stefanie for being upset. If his impulsiveness was causing her half as much frustration as it was giving him, she had every reason to want to strangle him.

He made up his bed on the couch and resigned himself to another long, lonely night.

Five

T.J. had no idea how long he'd slept when a huge clap of thunder woke him. Another crash followed almost immediately on the heels of the first, the sky flashing with jagged streaks of lightning, the wind howling like a malicious spirit.

Bolting upright, T.J. thought of Stefanie. He didn't know what to do. If she was awake, she would endure the storm alone rather than admit being afraid. He longed to go to her room and check on her, but didn't want her to think he was taking advantage of her vulnerability.

What he hoped was that Stefanie's bone-weariness would make her sleep through the cacophony. But it wasn't likely. He stood and pulled on his cotton robe to cover his nakedness, deciding to check on her, then stopped, once again unsure.

Suddenly, Stefanie flew from her room, her slender body lost in some kind of oversize pajama top, her hair tousled, her eyes glazed with fear and confusion. She looked right at T.J. but didn't seem to see him as she raced in his direction. "It's okay, it's okay," she was saying with soft urgency. "There's nothing to be afraid of." Reaching T.J., she tried to get past him, her voice suddenly edged with panic, though still a low whisper. "Where *are* you?" she cried. "Where did you go?"

"It's all right," T.J. said quietly, gently gathering her into his arms. "Everybody's fine, Steffie. There's no need to be frightened."

Stefanie stared at him, not sure where she was or why T.J. was holding her. "I'm not frightened," she protested, looking past him, trying to make sense of the jumbled images.

"You're not on the boat," T.J. said. "You're in an apartment with me, and you're safe."

"I know, but I have to find Morgan and Lisa and . . ." She paused, the truth beginning to filter through to her. "I—I guess I'm a little mixed up?"

T.J. cupped his hand behind her head and began stroking her hair, pressing his lips to her temple. "A little, babe."

"I'm not scared, Johnny," she said even as she nestled gratefully against T.J., her whole body shivering.

T.J. smiled fondly but sadly. It hurt him to see Stefanie frightened and even more to know she couldn't let go enough to admit it to him. "C'mon, babe," he said, gently leading her to the couch. As he stretched out with Stefanie beside him, he reflected that taking her back to her bed might have been more comfortable. But, sensing that she would resist having him join her there, he was willing to put up with being cramped.

"I'll stay for a minute," Stefanie said in a small voice, still barely awake, still trembling uncontrollably. But her body obeyed its own instincts, unable to resist the heat and strength T.J. offered as he entwined her bare, cold legs with his and he cradled her in the secure circle of his arms. "The thunder startled me, that's all," she insisted as she cuddled against him. "I was sound asleep, and it woke me up."

Holding her close, T.J. said, "I know, honey. It woke me up too."

A spasm gripped her body as more lightning sliced jaggedly through the sky and thunder exploded like an artillery barrage. T.J.'s arms tightened around her, and he tried to think of something soothing to say that wouldn't wound Stefanie's stubborn pride. "I have a confession, darlin'," he said at last, deciding that the best course would be to tease her. "I bribed the weatherman to cook up this storm so you'd come running to me. You see, the way I figured it, if all else failed—"

Stefanie gave a shaky laugh. "How silly. You're too much of a gentleman to take advantage of the situation anyway."

T.J. kissed her brows and eyelids, deeply contented by the realization that Stefanie had that much faith in him. And she was right. As much as he wanted her, as much as the elusive honey-almond fragrance in her hair tantalized his senses, as much as the soft curves pressed against his almost-naked body made the blood race through his veins, he would never make love to Stefanie when she was clinging to him out of fear. "Okay, so I'm not too bright," he said with mock sheepishness and a quiet chuckle.

Stefanie laughed again, breathing in the spicy scent that was so comfortingly familiar, feeling the heat of him permeating her body to dissolve her fears. Gradually, she felt her tense muscles letting go, and she drifted back to sleep.

Only after T.J. heard and felt Stefanie's deep, even breathing, did he notice that her pajama top was actually an old shirt of his, one he'd left behind when he'd packed hastily six months before.

He remembered something Stefanie had told him once, when he'd come home early from a four-day assignment to find her in bed, wearing his shirt. Oddly disconcerted, she'd laughed and cited community property rights, claiming his shirts were more comfortable than nightgowns.

But after they'd made love with the fierce need that had built up during their nights apart, she'd confessed that she always wore his clothes when he was away because they made her feel closer to him.

A lump suddenly lodged in his throat, and his eyes grew suspiciously moist. He vowed he would make it up to her for stupidly wasting the past six months. "I love you, baby," he whispered, hoping his words would penetrate into her dreams.

There had been a few occasions in Stefanie Sinclair's life when she'd hated herself in the morning.

Waking up in T.J.'s arms made for one of them.

Silently cursing her irrational fear of thunderstorms, she extricated herself from T.J.'s protective embrace, taking care not to wake him.

The apartment was quiet, the sky outside still dark, though the storm had ended. Stefanie crept down the hallway and into her room and checked her watch. It was just after five, and though Brad was an early riser, she remembered, even he wouldn't be up yet. At least he wouldn't know how she'd crawled onto the couch with T.J. like a terrified child.

But T.J. knew.

Stefanie didn't like anyone to see the chinks in her armor, even T.J.—especially T.J.—though she wasn't sure why. She got into bed and tried to catch a bit more sleep, but found herself brooding instead, thinking about the strange moment the night before, when she'd realized—along with T.J.—that she was trying her best to create argument out of nothing.

She knew she'd done it before. In fact, she kept running smack into the unpleasant possibility that she'd engineered the quarrel that had sent T.J. away. But why? She loved T.J. with all her heart. Why would she *try* to lose him?

Her reaction to the tuna boat bombing incident didn't make sense. No matter how many times and ways she looked at the situation, she couldn't fathom why she'd chosen to doubt T.J. when, in her heart, she'd known better.

Worse, she'd let him see her doubts. And then, with what she now considered the worst kind of unfaithfulness, she'd chosen not to tell him about seeing the picture in the tabloid that had aroused her ridiculous suspicions in the first place. Just as T.J. had said, she'd given him no chance to defend himself.

She'd used the sabotage of the boat to sabotage her marriage.

Rolling over onto her stomach and burying her face in the pillow, Stefanie was assailed by the memory of every dreadful word she'd said to T.J. on that last day. No wonder he'd thrown his clothes into a suitcase and slammed out of the apartment.

Sometimes, Stefanie thought, she wished *she* could walk out on that Stefanie Sinclair. The woman was an utter stranger to her.

At last, as streaks of lavender spread across the gray-blue sky, Stefanie made one important decision. Admitting to herself that she wasn't as invincible or in control of herself and events as she liked to pretend, she conceded that her habit of denying fears only made them grow and intensify. She ought to be more like Morgan, who confronted her every fear and methodically battled it into submission.

Getting out of bed, Stefanie faced herself in the mirror and blinked. Why *couldn't* she be more like Morgan? "Stefanie Sinclair," she said to her reflection, "it's time to stop hiding your head in the sand. Your big problem is that you're afraid of fear."

The trouble was, she had no idea how to conquer that particular phobia.

Perhaps, she thought, she should start smaller. With storms, for instance. What would Morgan do?

Immediately, Stefanie began making plans to accomplish her new, private goal, at the same time doing some vigorous stretching exercises, already feeling better about a lot of things.

Hungry and restless, Stefanie was grateful when she heard T.J. and Brad moving around and talking quietly. As she reached for her red silk kimono, she realized that T.J. must have noticed what she was using as a nightgown.

With a shake of her head, she swore quietly. Why didn't she just paint bleeding hearts all over her sleeve? Why was one part of her trying to advertise that she still loved him, while another part was battling that love? Why was she cursed with such confusion and perversity in her feelings for T.J.?

T.J. himself had told her: She was scared.

But the fear of being married to T.J. Carriere was another one that was too big to confront.

Stripping off his shirt, she put on her kimono and belted it tightly around her, gave her hair a punishing brushing, and padded out to face T.J., wondering if he would be in a cocky mood after having seen her at her most vulnerable. Yet even as the thought went through her mind, she knew she was up to her old tricks, being totally unfair to him. T.J. had given her no reason in the past to expect him to act that way.

"Good morning, gentlemen," she said as she breezed into the kitchen with a false smile, her heart skipping several beats when she glanced at T.J. It occurred to her that seeing him in the morning, or at any other time, inevitably made her pulse race, as if finding him in her life was a constant surprise and delight.

T.J. had been lifting a mug of coffee to his lips when Stefanie entered the room. He froze in place for several moments, taken aback by the sheer pleasure of looking at the woman.

His glance swept quickly over her, his eyes narrowing over the rim of his cup for only an instant as he saw that she'd changed from his shirt to a kimono that clung to her body in a way he'd have preferred to enjoy in private. T.J. didn't like her to be so alluring in front of another man, but he managed to hide his peevishness. "Morning, babe," he said at last, returning her smile, wondering how much she remembered of the previous night. He'd been disappointed to wake up and find that Stefanie had gone back to her own room, but he knew he should have expected it. She hated to be caught displaying any weakness. And in a way, he was glad she'd left him to wake up alone. It had been difficult enough to restrain his desire during the night, when tenderness had been his overriding emotion. In the early morning, he wasn't sure he could have resisted the temptation of her warm, pliant body.

"Hi, Mom," Brad said as he whipped up a batch of muffins. "Help yourself to the coffee."

"I'd rather have a shower first, if that's all right," she answered, feeling a flush creep over her skin thanks to T.J.'s bold scrutiny, which she recognized all too well. "Um . . . excuse me," she murmured, then hastily retreated, shocked that a mere look from T.J. could still arouse her so quickly.

By the time she'd returned to the kitchen, dressed in the taupe suit and black silk shell she'd worn the previous day, T.J. was alone. "Where's Brad?" she asked.

"He had to go to a meeting," T.J. answered. "You look great, Steffie. I like that outfit. You have a special kind of casual elegance all your own." He poured a cup of coffee for her and put warm muffins on two plates, then carried them to a small table for two in the corner of the kitchen. "Here, babe. Brad took the trouble to bake for us, so let's dig in."

"That was nice of him," Stefanie murmured, taking her place at the table despite the discomfort she felt at being part of the intimate domestic scene.

T.J. sat down opposite Stefanie and smiled. "Brad informed me that blueberry is your favorite. And he took care to point out that you take your coffee with cream, no sugar."

Stefanie frowned, wondering just how much trivial information the two men had shared about her while she'd been gone. "Unless your memory isn't what I think it is, you're fully aware of what kind of muffins I like and how I take my coffee."

"I know, but Brad seemed to get such a kick out of showing off *his* memory, I didn't have the heart to tell him I already knew."

Stefanie braced herself: Would T.J. mention the things he'd learned about her during the night when she'd gone running to him, wearing his shirt?

But T.J.'s thoughts were still on the man Stefanie had lived with. He heard himself voicing his nagging insecurities against his will. "Brad really is something, isn't he? He makes great pasta, whips up special salad dressings, bakes muffins, grinds his own coffee. Why wouldn't you have gotten interested in someone like that? Romantically interested, I mean."

Stefanie was oddly touched by the uneasiness she heard in his words. "If I were interested in a man for his culinary talents, I'd be a Paul Prudhomme groupie," she said with a teasing smile.

Though T.J. chuckled quietly, he couldn't help pressing the issue a little further. "It's just that you did live with Brad, and the two of you seem to get along so well."

"I think the reason we get along is that we never were romantically involved," Stefanie said. Then with sudden insight she added, "Are you being jealous, T.J., or wondering why I fell for you?"

He grinned. "Maybe a bit of both."

Stefanie hesitated, then made a childish face at him to dissipate the growing tenderness between them. She had to resist that tenderness. She wasn't ready for it. "Well, I'm not going to start cataloguing all your charms, so quit trying to pry them out of me," she said saucily. After another moment, she added, "Thanks for being so nice to me last night. I hope you aren't suffering with too many cramped muscles from having your couch invaded."

"My pleasure," he said, his voice suddenly husky with desire, his gaze dark and penetrating.

Stefanie had to steel herself against a sudden, tingling heat inside her. "And thanks for not mentioning anything until I brought up the matter," she added nervously.

T.J. grinned and finished his coffee. "Not mentioning what?"

With a laugh, Stefanie got to her feet and started tidying the kitchen. "You really can be a winning rogue, T.J. Carriere."

T.J. was glad she thought so. He only hoped he could be winning enough.

Stefanie had reason to be grateful to T.J. yet again when he managed to maneuver them through the airport crush and get them onto a flight to New Orleans.

But it troubled her that the two of them were becoming far too comfortable together, easing into their old husband and wife roles. He'd reverted to his habit of taking care of all the irritating details of travel, and she had lapsed into her uncharacteristic tendency of letting him do it. With anyone else but T.J., she automatically assumed responsibility.

Once again, he held her hand during the takeoff of the jet, his touch intensifying her sensual response to the moment. "It's that burst of power you enjoy," T.J. whispered, unable to resist teasing her.

Stefanie wished she hadn't told him her secret. "I admit I do like power," she said with a tight smile, deliberately misconstruing his remark.

He didn't let her get away with playing dumb. "Ah, babe, but in this case it's your surrender to power that thrills you."

"I believe I'll have coffee when the attendant comes around," Stefanie said, considering a retreat from the subject a good idea.

T.J. chuckled, knowing he'd scored his point. "You hate airline coffee," he reminded her. "I'm sure they have juice."

"Juice, then." Stefanie didn't care what she drank, as long as she'd managed to divert the path of T.J.'s thoughts. He was disturbingly attuned to feelings she herself barely acknowledged, and he knew the secrets of exciting her with subtle touches and provocative words that made her imagination wander into forbidden regions.

Aware of Stefanie's internal battle, T.J. took advantage of the moment. He patted her hand affectionately and leaned over to touch his lips to her cheek. "One of these days, darlin', you're going to admit to both of us how much you like to surrender occasionally. You know you can relinquish control without having the world crash in around you. You've done it. You haven't forgotten how it feels. And I'll be there for you, babe. That's a promise." Releasing her hand, he accepted a newspaper from the flight attendant, ordered Stefanie's juice, and blithely began reading.

Stefanie refused to think about his words. It was one thing for her to confess to herself that he might be right about her; it was another to admit it to him.

"Would you like part of the paper?" T.J. asked pleasantly.

"Yes, thank you," Stefanie answered. "The travel section, if you don't mind."

"So you're already back to work, are you?" he murmured as he handed over the pages.

"Already? I'm a day late. I just hope my business hasn't collapsed without me there to control it," she said with pointed irony.

T.J. merely chuckled, satisfied that his comments would invade Stefanie's mind whether she liked it or not.

"Are you going to stay with your parents?" Stefanie asked just before the plane landed in New Orleans.

"Will you invite me to stay with you?" he countered, expecting a quick negative.

Stefanie surprised him. "It's your apartment as much as mine, and there are two bedrooms. If you choose to stay there until we go through the legalities of our separation, I guess I really have nothing to say about it. Of course, I'd move out."

Though T.J. was disappointed that she was still talking as if divorce were inevitable, he admired her stern sense of fairness. "It's okay, babe. I've arranged for a furnished suite in an apartment hotel."

"I have some things of yours, you know," Stefanie said, trying to put some distance between herself and T.J. by talking as if the separation were final, though once again, she couldn't figure out her motives. The only thing she was certain of these days was that she was totally confused. "You left clothes, all your books, your stereo and tapes, that sort of thing. And, naturally, the furniture is as much yours as mine, so anything you want . . ."

T.J. hated what he was hearing. "I thought we were going to give ourselves a chance," he interrupted with a sharp edge to his voice.

"Well, we certainly won't be *living* together. I understood you to mean we might see each other occasionally, get to know each other, find out whether we're compatible. I'm merely suggesting that you might want to reclaim your possessions, and I'm trying to be fair about the things that are community property."

T.J. hated it when Stefanie hid behind formal speech. He felt like shaking her. But he restrained himself—and also managed to forego making a remark about the shirt she'd once called community property and was still wearing to bed at night. With what he considered his most patient tone, he said, "Babe, unless my stuff is in your way, let's just leave it where it is for now, okay?"

"Okay, fine. You don't have to bite my head off."

T.J. clenched his teeth, determined not to let her bait him, which she was obviously doing, whether or not she realized it. "Do up your seat belt," he muttered after a moment. "The sign's on."

"I didn't undo my seat belt in the first place," Stefanie said. "And I don't need minute-by-minute instructions from you on how to get through the simplest details of living."

Here we go again, T.J. thought, hearing the beginnings of one of their stupid quarrels. He cursed himself silently for falling into the trap. "I'm sorry," he forced himself to say. "You're right. I don't know why I nag you that way."

Stefanie blinked several times, staring at him. "I beg your pardon?"

He realized he'd thrown her a curve. "I find it difficult enough to apologize," he said with a little grin. "Don't ask me to repeat it."

"But you did apologize." Her voice was soft, her lips curved in a tiny smile—not one of triumph but one of pleased surprise and a bit of remorse. "I guess I don't have to be so touchy. I know you don't mean to suggest I'm a helpless dolt." She frowned again, wondering if she was giving in too easily. "Do you?"

"No, I don't," T.J. said, taking her hand in his. "It's just that you're precious to me, so I fuss over you when you don't want or need it." He took a sidelong glance at her middle. "Babe, are you *sure* you've done up that belt?"

Stefanie laughed, succumbing to his playful charm, beginning to wonder if it was possible that she and T.J. did have a chance. Perhaps she could forget about calling a lawyer just yet. In fact, hadn't she tacitly agreed to wait a while? She couldn't renege, could she?

As the plane touched down at the New Orleans airport, T.J.'s spirits plummeted. He knew that his effect on Stefanie would be diluted from there on. Her work would take precedence once more. She would have her own place, her own friends, her own life. He was going to have to scramble for any parcel of her time, yet he hoped to jump to the top spot on her list of priorities.

The signs of what was ahead started right away. T.J. wanted to see Stefanie home, but she said she was going straight to her office. "First, I plan to call my friend Mr. Gardner and give him an earful. Second, I have to look over some job applications. One of my riverboat gamblers has given his notice, and I have to find a replacement fast." She shook her head in discouragement. "I don't have high hopes, to be honest. I checked on Friday and the prospects were dismal, so I doubt whether the personnel agency has come up with any miracles so far today."

A germ of an idea began to form in T.J.'s brain. "Let's share a cab, shall we?"

"But we're going in opposite directions."

"Let's share one anyway," T.J. insisted, steering Stefanie out to the taxi stand.

Stefanie knew there was little sense arguing when T.J. had made a decision. Not all that eager to say good-bye anyway, she went along with him.

On the way to Stefanie's office, T.J. casually worked the conversation around to the subject of the employee she was losing. "Is this gambler really so important to your operation and so difficult to replace?"

Stefanie nodded. "The gambler isn't essential, but he adds a lot of atmosphere. And for part of the cruise he actually plays a few hands of poker with interested passengers. Whatever profits we make over and above the costs of the gambling operation go to charity, so the right person for the job has to be an expert at cards but strictly honest. The last thing we need is a shark who'll do something to make me lose my special license."

T.J.'s mind raced. "What other qualifications does this person need? Maybe I know someone who fills the bill."

"Well, we'd like someone who can be a bit of a showman, who can carry off the glamorous aura people associate with Hollywood, and he has to be great with people. It's a tough combination to find."

"You do give training, don't you?"

"Sure, but we have to have the raw material to work with."

T.J. nodded thoughtfully. "I'll keep the problem in mind," he promised.

Stefanie didn't have much hope that T.J. would be able to help find someone. He wasn't a card player himself, so he didn't have any poker partners he could suggest for the job. But it was sweet of him to take her concerns to heart. "I'm sure we'll come up with someone," she said, smiling at him. "If I'm really stuck, I'll get out my old costume and play the part of a lady gambler. I've done it many times before, when we were just getting started with the *Bayou Belle.*"

"You have enough of a work load," T.J. scolded automatically. "Being president of Dreamweavers, plus running your own branch of the company, is already a double job. Lisa told me that you've been spending even more hours at the office than when we were together, and you were doing too much then. And there's your environmental group. I don't know what you're trying to prove, Steffie. Why must you . . . ?" His voice trailed off as he saw her arched brow. "There I go again, right?"

Stefanie nodded but couldn't suppress a smile. "There you go again." The cab pulled up outside the building where Dreamweavers had its head office. "And here I go, back into the fray." Impulsively, she leaned over and kissed T.J.'s cheek, then hopped out of the cab before she forgot about work and pride and common sense, and simply threw herself into his arms as if love really could conquer all.

T.J. hated to let her go, but his reluctance was tempered by the knowledge that fate had given him an opening to pursue Stefanie in a way she wouldn't be able to turn down.

"What kind of job applicant?" Stefanie asked her secretary, Jody Richards, two days later as the younger woman stood looking at her with huge, startled doe eyes.

"He says he's interested in the riverboat gambler position," Jody said, biting her lip and pushing a cowlick of auburn hair out of her eyes. A slender, pale girl of about twenty, Jody was competent and pleasant, but she had a way of making Stefanie feel like a Valkyrie.

Stefanie was too pleased and puzzled about the possibility of having a suitable gambler drop into her lap to pay much attention to Jody's heightened level of anxiety. "That's strange," she murmured, more to herself than to Jody. "We haven't advertised the job, and the woman at the personnel agency didn't mention she was sending anyone over."

Jody cleared her throat, glancing back at the outer office, then warily eyed Stefanie again. "This . . . um . . . person claims he heard about it . . . um . . . through the grapevine."

"Why are you so skittish?" Stefanie asked with a little smile. "Have I been that difficult to live with the past couple of days?"

Jody gave a shaky laugh but said nothing.

Stefanie's smile faded to a frown. She knew she'd been in a rotten mood ever since she'd left T.J. in that cab, but she didn't realize she'd taken out her feelings on her staff. "I'll see the man right away," she told the girl. "And if I've been a pain, I'm sorry."

Jody stared at her for a moment, then said in a tiny voice, "You're never a pain, Stefanie. You're really nice. It's just that—" She swallowed hard, then hurried away.

Frowning, Stefanie swiveled in her chair to look out the large window behind her desk, drumming a pencil against the palm of her hand as she stared almost unseeingly across the street at the swath of green that was a corner of City Park.

Suspecting that she might have been more abrupt with Jody than the girl was admitting, Stefanie berated herself for her self-absorbed behavior. T.J. obviously had too much effect on her, if she could terrorize her secretary into stuttering.

Hearing Jody showing the man in, Stefanie turned to greet the applicant. Her mouth stayed open exactly where she'd started to form a word, her pencil clicking as it dropped to her desk, her eyes widening as she burst into helpless, delighted laughter.

"Hi, babe," T.J. said with a wicked grin.

Six

After several moments of total silence, Stefanie recovered her poise and spoke carefully to Jody. "This is the applicant?"

The girl nodded with the jerky motions of a bird pecking at a tree trunk.

"No wonder you were a nervous wreck," Stefanie said, feeling sorry for her secretary. Jody had been with her a year and had met T.J. several times, so she'd known all along who the job seeker was. Obviously T.J. had told the girl not to spill the beans. "Never mind, Jody. I don't hold you responsible for T.J. Carriere's capers."

Gratefully, Jody smiled and scooted back to her own office, closing the door and leaving T.J. and Stefanie alone in the room that usually seemed quite spacious to Stefanie but all at once struck her as tiny and crowded. Sometimes she forgot how tall T.J. was, how imposing.

She hoped that neither the sudden flush creeping over her skin nor the violent beating of her heart under her red silk blouse nor the leap of her pulse throbbing wildly in a vein at her temple were too noticeable.

Decked out in a black suit, ruffled white shirt, brocade vest, string tie, polished black cowboy boots, and a wide-brimmed black hat, T.J. was devastating. He was the ultimate riverboat gambler: Tyrone Power, James Garner, and Clark Gable all rolled into one gorgeous male. He filled the room with an aura of excitement.

But Stefanie wasn't prepared to admit how dramatically he affected her. "This isn't fair, T.J.," she scolded. "You arouse my hopes about finding an honest, competent gambling man, and what do I see? A nutty ex-husband who has to cheat at solitaire to win."

"I'm your husband, not your ex-husband," T.J. said pleasantly, taking off his hat and tossing it with unerring accuracy to a brass rack in the corner before moving toward her desk. "And you are looking at the *Bayou Belle*'s newest resident gambler—on a temporary basis, mind you. I'm here to bail you out, ma'am."

Stefanie shook her head and gave in to another bout of laughter.

T.J.'s expression was slightly wounded. "This is no joke, darlin'."

Stefanie was blinking back tears of mirth and, she was loath to admit, tears of joy at seeing T.J. again, even under such ludicrous circumstances. Ever since he'd driven off in the cab, she'd caught herself watching the phone, hoping he would call. But this ploy of his was unbelievable. "You expect me to take you seriously?"

"Unless you want to be accused of unfair employment practices, babe, you have to take me seriously."

"T.J., I told you, this job requires a person to be an expert card player! You're talking to Stefanie, remember? You can't bluff your way through this one."

"I don't intend to try to bluff you. Give me an audition."

"What do you mean an audition? Okay, I admit you look the part, and I know you're great with people when you want to be, but you're a writer. An environmentalist. You're no cardsharp. You couldn't play a decent game of Go Fish to save your life, so why don't you give up this silly charade right now?"

"Steffie, you've told me you need a riverboat gambler. I just happen to be available for a few weeks, because the assignments I have on my plate at the moment are so tame, I could do them in my sleep—or at least on my lap-top in my spare time. As I've already told you, I'd like a change of pace from all the serious concerns I've been involved in for the past few years. Maybe I'll even do an article: "I Was a Mississippi Gambler for the F.B.I.," or some such thing. The point is, there's a position open with your company, and I'm honestly applying for it. Now, are you going to give me a chance or not? A few hands of poker ought to be a fair test of my skills."

Stefanie regarded him thoughtfully for a while, realizing that T.J. might well be the answer to more than one of her problems.

Suddenly, she cleared everything off her desk and buzzed her secretary. "Hold all my calls, will you Jody? I'll be in conference for a while."

T.J. pulled a tan leather chair closer to Stefanie's

desk, sat down, and slapped a deck of cards on the polished teak surface.

Stefanie shook her head. "Come on, T.J.," she said with a little laugh as she opened her desk drawer to take out a rack of poker chips and a sealed pack of cards. "I didn't call you on your two-headed coin trick in Key West, but you'll understand if I prefer to use a fresh deck, won't you?"

"Fine by me, darlin'," T.J. said, pocketing his cards. "Just so you promise that I get the job if I can whup you at this game."

"Whup *me*?" Stefanie repeated in utter disbelief. "Now really, I don't expect you to go that far, Mr. Carriere. A decent showing will earn you the position."

T.J. smiled. "Darlin', I said I'd whup you at cards, and that's what I'm planning to do."

Stefanie laughed again, but with a bit less hilarity. Something in T.J.'s manner told her not to be too sure of herself.

How silly, she thought impatiently. T.J. couldn't have turned himself into a poker player in two days. It wasn't his game.

As she handed him the deck to open, she found herself wondering just what *was* his game.

He put the opened deck on the table. "Cut for deal, babe?"

"High card?" Stefanie asked as she lifted off about a quarter of the deck.

Nodding, T.J. put his thumb and third finger on either side of the remaining cards, his forefinger in the middle of the top one, and picked up another section of the deck.

Stefanie smiled as she showed him her card.

T.J.'s smile was broader. "Well now, imagine that.

Jack of hearts for you, queen of hearts for me. I'd say that's an interesting omen, wouldn't you?"

"Your deal," Stefanie said, taken aback by the cut, wondering whether T.J. had managed somehow to cheat, even with her deck. The jack and queen of hearts seemed too coincidental to be genuine. Unless . . .

Stefanie gave herself a mental shake to drive out the teasing memory of Heather's claims of fated love.

T.J. shuffled the deck, tapped one end of it on the desk, cut it, and riffled the cards together, then shuffled a few more times, his motions easy and relaxed.

Anyone could learn to shuffle a deck, Stefanie told herself, dividing up the poker chips.

"Name your poison, darlin'," T.J. said cheerfully.

Stefanie stifled a giggle, enjoying his act. "I suppose you'd like one of those sissy games like Deuces and Jacks and the Man With the Ax Are Wild?"

T.J. gave her the crooked grin she remembered too well. It usually meant trouble. "How about a little game of Five Card Stud Showdown, one down and four up?"

This time Stefanie couldn't suppress her chuckle of delight. T.J. certainly had learned his lines. "What are the stakes?" she asked.

His answer was unhesitating. "All chips have equal value, three-chip limit to open, three-bump maximum."

Stefanie's laughter died in her throat. She gaped at T.J. as if he were a stranger. "You have a lot of confidence, cowboy. Do you expect to be able to raise me three times?"

"I'm just trying to avoid any surprises, babe. It'll be hard enough beating you as it is."

He was putting her on, Stefanie thought. He'd picked up the right things to say, but there was no way he could have learned the game. No way at all. She smiled, trying to ignore the electric current T.J.'s looks and manner were sending through her. "Deal."

T.J. placed the cards in front of her. "Don't you want to cut 'em?"

Stefanie tapped the top of the deck twice with her middle finger to signal that she trusted him to deal the cards as shuffled.

T.J. picked up the cards and dealt one to each of them, face down

Stefanie looked at her card. It was a three. *Not a great start,* she thought without much concern, keeping her expression impassive. Taking a chip, she tossed it to the center of the desk. "I'll open."

T.J. looked at his card, then threw in a chip. "I'll see you." He dealt the second card to each of them, face up.

Stefanie's card was a five, T.J.'s a three. Normally, Stefanie thought, she would not add another chip. But she couldn't resist being more aggressive with T.J. just to see what he'd do. She wondered how long he could sustain his performance. Quite a while, she suspected by what he'd said and done so far. Her already enormous admiration for him leapt by several notches. She tipped two chips into the pot, saying quietly, "Bet two."

T.J. studied both the upcards, then looked at his downcard, then at Stefanie. "I'll see you . . ." He put in two chips, smiled, and added two more. "And raise you."

Without missing a beat, Stefanie tossed in two more of her own. "Call." T.J. was perfect, she thought, beginning to hope he actually knew what he was doing. If he did, he *could* bail her out until she found a permanent replacement for her gambler—and until she'd found out whether Stuart Gardner's barely veiled threats to give her a few business hassles of her own were empty.

T.J. turned up their next cards, a four to Stefanie, another three to himself.

Beginner's luck, Stefanie told herself. T.J had a pair, and so far, she had nothing much, except perhaps the start of a straight. "Your threes are high, so it's your bet," she said, in case he didn't know.

He looked at her upcards carefully, then at her, then smiled and spoke with a lazy drawl. "I do believe it's time to separate the men from the girls, ma'am." He tossed three chips into the pot. "I'll bet three."

He knows exactly how to bug me, Stefanie thought, amused at his obvious ploy, yet slightly shaken by his move, and definitely excited by his bold challenge. "Make it six," she said, putting in her chips. T.J. was hoping to turn up another three to add to his pair, she reasoned. The odds were against it, when only one was left in the deck. And he didn't know whether she actually had a pair. It was a crucial moment for him. She wondered what he'd do: Fold, call, or raise.

To her surprise, he raised three more, then gave her a smile of sublime innocence.

He'd turned the tables, Stefanie thought, her pulse rate accelerating. The man was proving himself a worthy opponent. She was left with no option but to raise. If she didn't, T.J. would know her down card didn't match any of her others. She threw in six chips. "I believe there's one more bump available, so I'll see *your* three and raise you three more."

T.J. grinned. "As usual, babe, I'm at your beck and . . . call." He tossed in three more chips, then dealt two face-up cards—a seven to Stefanie, a ten to himself. He studied the five-four-seven sequence in front of her. "A possible straight, babe. Not bad." He stroked his chin thoughtfully. "Now, if I remember correctly, I'd need three of a kind and a pair to beat you, wouldn't I?"

Stefanie wasn't sure whether he was playing dumb or ribbing her. "Also known as a full house or a tight," she informed him, her breathing suddenly uneven, her gaze caught for a long moment as a blue flame in his soft green eyes mesmerized her.

"Right," he said after several seconds, blinking slowly. "Tell you what, darlin'. We went sort of heavy on the betting the last hand. I'm going to see where you're coming from. I'll just check. No bet this time."

Stefanie smiled sweetly, battling the spell he was casting over her. "I won't take advantage of you, T.J. I'll just check too. Deal the cards."

He nodded. "Okay, babe. Last ticket."

To her amazement, Stefanie felt as if she had her life savings at stake. T.J.'s sure-of-himself manner was making the blood pound in her head until she was almost dizzy.

He turned up a six for her, another ten for himself.

Stefanie's heart drummed faster and faster. She'd played a lot of poker in her time; never had a session given her such a deep, visceral thrill. She forced herself to think about the hand. T.J.'s two pair weren't good enough to beat her straight. But what was his down card?

T.J. was still high, so again it was his bet. He took

his time about looking at her cards, his eyes twinkling, his grin amused and confident. "You wouldn't have a three under there, would you, babe?"

For the first time in all her years of playing poker, Stefanie couldn't keep her deadpan expression. The ghost of a triumphant smile quivered at the corners of her mouth. "Your bet, T.J."

He sat back in his chair, his long legs stretched out to the side, his ankles crossed, the deck of cards held at chest level by the fingers of both hands, his thumb riffling the edges in a contemplative rhythm, his gaze fixed on Stefanie's eyes as if he were trying to read her mind. Or, she wondered, as her thoughts became fuzzy, as if he—like some potent drug—were trying to alter her mind.

She feared he could do it. A heaviness was seeping into her limbs, a languor that pervaded every part of her. Her mouth felt dry; she moistened her lips with her tongue, then cursed herself for betraying emotion. It was unforgivable for the poker player she prided herself on being.

But poker wasn't the only game going on, and Stefanie suspected T.J. was winning at both. She'd never seen him so mysteriously exciting.

Finally he broke the tense silence. "Listen, babe. With hands like these, I know you're going to bump me to the limit. So let's skip the preliminaries and bet all twelve chips at once." He pushed his chips toward the pot.

Stefanie was caught completely off guard. Her quick intake of breath surprised her. After all, she reminded herself, there was no financial risk to the game, and this hand was only the first of many. But she'd never been quite as stunned by another player's daring move as by T.J.'s. Meeting his gaze as steadily as she could manage, she murmured, "See you," and pushed twelve chips to the center.

T.J. nodded. "It's your show, babe."

Stefanie flipped over her down card, certain she'd called his bluff.

He looked at the three she'd just turned up. "You *did* have the little devil! Good for you." Then he reached for his down card. "The thing is, my hole card happens to be a ten, which gives me three of a kind and a pair." He grinned. "Which, as you pointed out, would be called a full house or a tight and beats your straight."

Stefanie gaped at him in shock. Somehow the man had done it. He'd . . . *whupped* her on the first hand. "Where did you learn to play poker?" she asked with astonishment.

"Well now, I did mention all those long northern nights, didn't I? A man needs something to pass the time, and there was always a deck of cards handy."

Stefanie briskly gathered up the cards, prepared to enjoy what was ahead. She still believed she could outplay T.J. over the long haul, but he was going to give her a run for her money. "I believe it's my deal," she said, barely controlling the charged excitement pulsing inside her, remembering too late that only T.J. could make her feel such sizzling heat—and even he had never turned up the voltage quite this high.

They had played for two hours. T.J. had won all the chips but three. Stefanie knew her concentration wasn't what it should be. When she ought to have been thinking about the cards, she kept catching herself staring at his hands, the fingers long and tapered and graceful yet strong looking and utterly masculine. Memories of pleasures those hands had given her in the past kept washing over her, filling her body with intoxicating warmth, like the effects of strong brandy.

The fifth card had been dealt, and they were down to the last bump allowed.

Stefanie suspected that T.J. had another winning hand—though he could be bluffing. It was hard to tell with him. Impossible, in fact. Especially when she couldn't keep her mind off the lean hardness of the male body across from her, the tempting mouth, the fascinating eyes.

She could fold, she thought, nudging her attention back to the game. But she had a pretty fair hand herself and folding at such a moment wasn't her style. The hand had to be played out. "Bet three," she said, tossing in her last chips.

T.J. plucked at his lower lip, studying his cards. He picked up three chips. "Call," he said, hesitated for just an instant, then put in three more. "And raise."

Stefanie drew a deep breath and let it out slowly. She couldn't believe it. T.J. had won. Just as he'd said he would, he'd whupped her not just for one hand but for the whole bundle. "I guess I'm finished," she said with a note of stunned amazement in her voice. "No more chips."

T.J. smiled. "Did you think I'd be a southern gentleman and be satisfied just to call?"

"You know better than to believe I'd expect special treatment," Stefanie answered

"Babe, I don't like it to end this way. Couldn't I advance you the three chips you need so we can play the hand out, winner take all?"

Her interest was caught. "Why would you do that?"

"Maybe I'm a southern gentleman after all, darlin'. But let's say I get the riverboat job, win or lose."

"Agreed," Stefanie said. She'd made that decision after the first few hands. "Any other conditions?"

"You give me a marker for the three chips. Win or lose, I keep them to claim later, one at a time. And I get the job."

Stefanie shook her head and laughed. "The chips aren't worth anything. We weren't playing for money, and you've got the job, so what would you be claiming?"

T.J.'s whole expression suddenly became challenging, his voice low and caressing. "Whatever I say the chips represent when I decide to collect on 'em, babe."

Stefanie blinked slowly, laughing again, this time nervously. "Why would I agree to such a blank-check arrangement?"

"Because it's the only way you still have a chance to beat me," T.J. said smoothly. "And you do want to beat me, don't you?"

He knew her so well, Stefanie thought, her gaze locked on his. Fully aware of how it killed her to lose a game, he was going to force her right to the wall. She was supposed to sign a marker without knowing what he intended to collect? She'd be out of her mind to do that, even if the silly slip of paper would be meaningless.

Except that it wouldn't be meaningless, she reminded herself. She wouldn't welsh.

On the other hand, she suddenly thought, perhaps she should sign the marker. Perhaps there was a bigger issue at stake than a few poker chips. What better way to show T.J. she was capable of trusting him after all? Not that much trust was involved. T.J. wouldn't hold her to anything that she truly couldn't honor. Not T.J. Carriere. He was a tease, but he was, indeed, a southern gentleman of the first order.

Stefanie reached for her memo pad, scrawled an IOU, signed it, and pushed it toward T.J., laughing softly. "You're crazy, you know that?"

"I'm crazy?" he said, tucking the paper into his inside jacket pocket. "You're the one who signed an open-ended IOU, babe."

"Let's finish the game," she said as T.J. dropped three chips into her upturned palm. "I'm calling your raise, so let's see where we stand." She tossed the three chips onto the pile. With four cards in each hand face up on the table, Stefanie found herself with a pair of eights to T.J.'s pair of fives—unless he had another five in the hole. Judging by his run of luck so far, it was entirely possible that he did.

But he abruptly folded his hand and threw down his cards, gathering them in with the rest of the deck. "That finishes me," he said without emotion. "Your eights beat my fives. You called my bluff."

A burst of adrenaline shot through Stefanie. She'd won!

A moment later she was suspicious. "Why didn't you show me your down card?" she asked.

"I didn't know I was supposed to," T.J. answered, totally unruffled.

"It's not required," Stefanie admitted. "But why didn't you? How do I know you didn't throw the game for some weird reason? How can I be certain I won?"

T.J. stood, walked around to Stefanie's side of the desk, and took her hand in both of his, turning it as he bent to touch his lips, then the tip of his tongue, to her palm.

The gentle kiss sent tiny, unbearably intense thrills swirling through Stefanie's whole body. She felt a flush creep over her skin and knew T.J. could see it at the open neck of her blouse. She didn't care.

"You *can't* be certain you won, darlin'," T.J. said quietly. "But does it matter, when the game is just between us?"

Stefanie almost stopped breathing. She had no answer.

With an indolent smile, T.J. reached down to the pile of chips with his free hand and put three of them in his vest pocket.

Stefanie watched, fascinated, her heart pounding as she wondered what value T.J. was going to place on those chips.

"So when do I start my new job, darlin'?" he asked.

"Monday, if that's suitable," Stefanie said, trying without much success to sound businesslike. "Come here to the office around ten. You'll have a week of training, at first here, then on the *Bayou Belle*." She couldn't suppress a wry, worried smile. "I do a lot of the training. Somehow I can't see you taking well to this situation, but if you're willing to give it a try, then I am too."

"Just snap out those orders, boss lady," he said with a grin, still holding her hand with a sensual tenderness and confident authority that belied his words. "I'm yours to command."

"Would that it were so," Stefanie muttered.

T.J. laughed, bent to capture her lips in a kiss that increased her doubts about his sincere willingness to treat her as his employer, then stood and walked jauntily away. "See you Monday, babe."

She was taken aback. Monday? Didn't he want to see her over the weekend? What was he up to *now*? "By the way," she said coolly, "I assume you rented that outfit for this audition of yours. We'll get you fitted with some things from our wardrobe department."

"Sure," T.J. answered laconically. "But I didn't rent these duds. I bought them. Like you said, I had a lot of confidence." With a wink and a wicked grin, he turned and was gone.

Stefanie sat back in her chair, shaking her head slowly in disbelief at the infernal cockiness of the man.

Then she closed her eyes and wondered how she was going to be able to wait until Monday morning to see him again.

Seven

T.J. showed up at ten sharp on Monday morning, once again dressed in his gambler outfit.

When he walked into Stefanie's office, her stomach tightened into a knot. The man was maddeningly attractive, but she was miffed. In her opinion, T.J. had a strange way of trying to promote a reconciliation. The whole weekend had gone by, and she hadn't received so much as a phone call from him.

T.J. pulled up a chair and sat opposite Stefanie, noticing the strain in her eyes. He wondered if her weekend had been as long and lonely and restless as his. Dozens of times he'd come close to phoning her, yet he'd fought the impulse. Being pushy and impetuous didn't seem like the right way to start building the relationship he wanted with her.

For a moment, he said nothing. During the past months he'd wished so often that he could see Stefanie, it seemed only right to take a few soul-satisfying moments to drink in her loveliness, to breathe in her tantalizingly elusive floral scent. In a tailored silk dress the color of daffodils, her lustrous hair caught back on one side with an enameled comb, her lips pink and full and tempting, she surpassed even his most vivid dreams of her. "You look like a bright spring morning," he said at last.

Stefanie resisted the melting sensations inside her. "I see we're off to a businesslike start."

"Let me try again. I did forget myself for a minute, didn't I?" T.J. said, raising himself slightly from his chair and lifting his hat. "You look like a bright spring morning, *ma'am*, you surely do."

A smile curved Stefanie's lips. "I have a feeling you're going to be absolutely incorrigible, T.J. Carriere. By the way, you don't have to wear the costume during training."

"I don't? That's too bad. I was starting to like it. But I guess you're right. Still, I think I'll wear the hat just to get used to it. I wouldn't want another lapse like that one a minute ago, forgetting to take it off to a lady and all."

"Heaven forbid," Stefanie murmured, then chewed on her lower lip, wondering how T.J. was going to react to what she was about to tell him. "T.J., before you start the training, there's something I should have told you last week. It might make you think twice about taking this job."

"If it was anyone but you talking, babe, I'd wonder if you were looking for a way to renege on our deal."

"I'm not reneging. But . . . well . . ."

"Blurt it out, darlin'. It's the easiest way," T.J. said with a quizzical smile.

"All right. You remember that Stuart Gardner visited my office while I was away?"

T.J. nodded, keeping his expression deadpan despite the anticipation buzzing through him. Was Stefanie about to confide in him?

Stefanie was tempted to exact a promise from T.J. that he wouldn't blow his top but quickly discarded the idea. Nothing was more maddening to T.J.—or, for that matter, to her—than a "now don't get mad" preamble. She chose to barrel ahead and hope for the best. "Gardner says he's sick of interference in his business, sick of seeing his company maligned by the media, and most of all, sick of the sudden interest being taken by government officials in his company's waste disposal methods. He has suggested rather strongly that I persuade my environmental group to back off."

T.J.'s eyes narrowed. "How strongly did he make that suggestion, Steffie?"

"There were no personal threats," Stefanie answered hastily. "But Gardner has hinted broadly that he could fight fire with fire."

"Meaning?"

"He didn't say. I hope he's all talk, but I suspect he'll try to make trouble for the *Bayou Belle*. It wouldn't take much effort to cast doubt on the integrity of my gambling operation and jeopardize my special license. The cruise would go on, but the publicity would be less than pleasant."

T.J. spoke very carefully. "Are you warning me not to cheat, Stefanie?"

She frowned, surprised to find that she didn't like T.J. to use her proper name. It sounded cold and formal from him. And the furrows in her forehead deepened as she belatedly realized that she'd given T.J. the wrong impression about what she was driving at. "I know you wouldn't cheat," she said quietly. "The jibes we trade in private and the serious business of my gambling operation are two different matters. The truth is, when you walked in here last week and proved to me you could do the job, and insisted you wanted it, you were like the cavalry arriving in the nick of time. I'm wary of hiring anyone. How can I know the new gambler wouldn't do something stupid, or even deliberately dishonest because he's secretly on Gardner's payroll? The man would love to catch us in an infraction or entrap us if necessary."

T.J. stared at Stefanie in pleased shock. "Are you saying you feel you can count on me not to be stupid or dishonest?"

"Of course," Stefanie said without hesitation, sorry that T.J. was surprised by her faith in him. "But in all fairness, you have to know what you might be up against. I'm not sure why you wanted this job . . ."

"Baby, don't play dumb," T.J. said with a slight gruffness that was meant to hide the depth of his emotions. He'd been certain that the biggest obstacle to rebuilding a marriage with Stefanie was her lack of trust in him. Apparently he was wrong. "You know I just want to be close to you," he added, managing a smile.

"How would I know, when you haven't called me?" Stefanie shot back, caught with her defenses down.

T.J. gaped at her, amazed all over again. "I had the impression you didn't want to hear from me, babe."

Shifting in her chair, Stefanie shuffled papers around on her desk, cursing herself under her breath for showing her feelings so blatantly. What was the matter with her? "I didn't. Anyway, back to the point. Do you want the job, knowing the possible difficulties?"

"I want it," T.J. said quietly. "And thanks for the vote of confidence."

Stefanie rolled her eyes. "Are you kidding? Thank *you* for being here when I need someone I can trust. And I do trust you, T.J. You'll play it straight, you'll learn and follow the rules, you'll protect my interests." She allowed herself to grin as she decided not to swell T.J.'s head too much. "Just don't get mad if you think someone's baiting you, okay? A brawl on the *Bayou Belle* wouldn't do much for our family-oriented image, so hold your temper at all costs."

"At all costs," T.J. agreed, happier than he'd been in a long time.

Stefanie buzzed her secretary, abruptly deciding she needed to put some distance between herself and T.J.'s charm for a little while.

When Jody entered the office, she gave T.J. the same perplexed look he'd seen on her face when he'd walked past her desk a while earlier. "Hi," she said in a small voice.

Stefanie smiled, realizing that the girl hadn't been told that T.J had gotten the job. "Jody, would you please take our new gambler down to the wardrobe department and tell Meg to fit him out?"

T.J. frowned. "Is there something wrong with this getup?"

"It's perfect," Stefanie answered. "But you can't get along with just one suit, can you? A Mississippi gambler has to be a regular dandy."

T.J. was sobered by her comment. It brought home the fact that he really had gotten himself a day-in, day-out job of dealing with tourists who would expect him to be pleasant no matter how he felt or how they acted—not to mention possibly hostile passengers, hired to look for trouble.

He followed Jody to a room down the hall, musing that he must love Stefanie an awful lot to have gotten himself a job playacting.

After being fussed over, measured, and pinned for what felt like forever, he was released just before noon and went back to Stefanie's office. "Is the boss lady still in?" he asked Jody.

The girl bit her lip. "Yes, but she asked me to get you to fill out some forms."

"What forms?"

Jody shrugged. "The usual employment data." She handed over a thick sheaf of papers and a pen.

"I guess I've been a free-lancer so long, I'd forgotten what foolishness a person has to go through these days for the privilege of taking a simple job." T.J. leafed through the endless forms, then looked at Stefanie's closed door. "Am I supposed to wait to be announced whenever I want to see Madame President, or can I just go in?"

"Stefanie said for you to go right in when you've finished . . ." Jody's voice trailed off and her mouth remained open as T.J. headed for Stefanie's office, blank forms in hand.

He pushed open the door of the inner sanctum, closed it behind him, and covered the distance to Stefanie's desk in three long strides. Brandishing the papers, he gave her a pleasant smile. "What the hell's all this, darlin'?"

Stefanie was unruffled as she looked up at him. She'd expected his reaction. T.J. didn't take kindly to red tape. "Didn't Jody explain?"

"Employment data, she called it. I'm filling in temporarily here, babe. Bailing you out, remember? I'm not looking for an old-age pension and six days sick leave a year, and you do not need my educational background, work experience and medical history."

"I knew you'd make a fuss," Stefanie said half to herself, barely suppressing a grin. "Are you saying you refuse to fill out the usual forms?"

"That's the picture, babe. Look, I don't even want you to pay me—"

"I have to pay you, T.J. I won't accept your help otherwise. Besides, the government has passed very good laws about giving people a day's pay for a day's work."

T.J. shook his head in disgust. "Governments. They're always poking their noses into every place but where they ought to be. Tell you what. I'll work the job as a research assignment for an article. Maybe I'll do a series of pieces about offbeat careers. I know an editor who loves that sort of thing. Who could complain about that arrangement?"

Stefanie considered his offer but rejected it. "You could pick up all the research material you wanted in a few days, but I might need you much longer than that." Too late she realized the double meaning in her words and saw a mischievous grin begin to light up T.J.'s face.

"I hope you will, darlin'," he said. "I truly hope you will."

Stefanie shook her head in mostly feigned despair. "As a riverboat gambler, I mean."

"Okay, give me the training. Then I'll spend, say, two weeks working the cruise. After that, if you still haven't found a permanent replacement, we can talk money. But it'll be a free-lance contract, Steffie. None of this employment garbage." To illustrate the point, he dropped the papers into her wastebasket.

After a moment's thought, Stefanie nodded. "The training plus one week, not two. That's plenty of time for your research. After that, you get paid using a free-lance contract."

"You've got yourself a deal," T.J. said, thrusting out his hand.

"I'll have to check with the bureaucrats to make sure I'm not breaking some rule or other before I shake on this agreement," Stefanie said with a bit of a scowl.

T.J. grabbed her hand. "C'mon, babe. I'm your husband. Can't I pitch in and help my wife with her business, even in this law-crazy country? And if I can't, and you are doing something illegal, what's the problem? I'd be the chief witness against you, and a husband can't testify against his wife. So it's settled."

Stefanie gave in. "I just remembered what kept me off balance when we were together. Having you in my life is like being an animal tamer with a ring full of well-behaved lions and one maverick tiger."

T.J. kept her hand in his. "And you'd love to be able to crack your whip at the maverick and see him jump?"

"I'm not sure," Stefanie said pensively. "Maybe I like him just the way he is."

T.J. grinned and walked around to her side of the desk, still holding her hand. He pulled her to her feet and drew her close to him. "There's no maybe about it, darlin'. You need a maverick tiger around to keep you on your toes."

"To keep me on tenterhooks, you mean," Stefanie

scolded without much conviction. "I never know what you're going to do next."

"You can't stay in control, huh?"

"Exactly. And I do like to be in control, remember? There's no sense pretending otherwise."

He slid his arms around her. "In control of what, babe?"

"Of my business, my time, my . . . social calendar, my life, myself . . ."

"Of the response of your body," T.J. added in a teasing tone. "Of the organization of your home, of the safety of your community, of the future of killer whales, of the economic summit talks, of the course of the sun, of the rhythm of the tides . . ." He smiled innocently. "Have I left out anything?"

"I should fire you," Stefanie said, unable to sound as cross as she'd like.

"You can't. There are very good laws against wrongful dismissal. Let's have lunch."

"Incorrigible," Stefanie muttered.

"It's a nice day. Let's have a picnic. We can take my car, pick up sandwiches somewhere, and sit on the shore of Lake Pontchartrain, like we used to."

Stefanie's lips curved in a slow smile. "I packed sandwiches this morning. Your favorites: chicken on whole wheat bread smothered in mayonnaise."

"And beer?" T.J. asked, his heart skipping every second beat. He hadn't expected Stefanie to be so helpful.

With a tilt of her head to indicate the minifridge in the corner of her office, Stefanie answered, "Ice cold."

"Has anyone ever told you you're the most fantastic woman who ever lived?"

"Yes. You. Whenever I offered you an ice-cold beer. I warn you, T.J., this will be a working lunch. I'm going to start briefing you on the background of our gambling-for-charity operation. And as you now know, that's a pile of red tape you *can't* ignore."

"I'm all yours, boss. Fill my stomach with chicken sandwiches and beer, and I'll let you fill my head with bureaucratic rules to your heart's content."

"T.J., I'm serious—"

He stopped her words with a gentle but thorough kiss. "Baby, I thought you said you could count on me. Have you changed your mind?"

Stefanie took a deep breath. "No."

Rubbing his nose against hers, he grinned. "Then there's no problem. So let's get on with our working picnic." As he released her, he laughed.

"What's so funny?" Stefanie asked, moving to get the sandwiches and beer from the fridge.

"Only my Steffie could come up with such a contradiction in terms. A working picnic. I have to hand it to you, babe. It's a first for me."

She stuck out her tongue at him, stuffed the lunch into an insulated bag she'd brought along, and handed it to him. Grabbing her purse, she opened the office door. "Shall we go?"

True to his southern gentleman code, he replaced her hand with his on the doorknob and made a sweeping bow. "After you, babe."

Jody looked up, her big eyes full of questions.

"It's all right about the forms," Stefanie said pleasantly. "Mr. Carriere and I have . . . come to an arrangement."

The first arrangement of many, T.J. thought, if he had his way.

•   •   •   •

The week sped by in a blur as T.J. learned what was expected of a Dreamweaver's, Inc. employee and of a gambler on the *Bayou Belle.* It involved more than card playing, he discovered, though knowing every poker variation that might be thrown at him was part of the job.

"Maybe I should grow a mustache," he suggested during one of the card sessions Stefanie put him through. "What do you think, babe? Would it give me that devil-may-care look?"

"You're blessed with quite enough of a devil-may-care look," Stefanie said, beginning to have second thoughts about turning him loose on a ship filled with females looking for romance.

She was more off balance with T.J. than ever. He was flirtatious with her but seemed more interested in learning the job than in patching up their marriage. He didn't try to see her in the evenings and didn't show the slightest sign of disappointment or jealousy or even curiosity on the two occasions when she'd had appointments and couldn't have lunch with him.

He grinned as he won another hand. "Your mind's wandering again, Steffie," he scolded mildly.

She threw down her cards in disgust. "I should send all my gamblers up north to pose as bear poachers."

"It wasn't the north or posing as a poacher that made me learn poker," T.J. said softly. "It was needing some way—any way—to feel close to you when we were so far apart."

To Stefanie's dismay, her eyes filled with tears. T.J. was far too adept at arousing instant emotional responses in her. Abruptly she stood up. "Let's take a look at the diagram of the paddle wheeler. As a staff member, even a free-lance one, you have to know every bit of it like a book, for the sake of safety."

"Won't I get to know the physical layout next week when we go aboard the *Bayou Belle*?"

"Of course, but the more you know in advance, the more quickly you'll become oriented."

T.J. shrugged and got to his feet. "Whatever you say, boss lady."

"I wish you'd quit calling me that!"

"Okay, babe. I didn't know it bothered you."

"So does *babe*. And darlin', and all the rest of the pet names you use."

T.J. crooked his finger under her chin and forced her to look at him. "Tell me another one, darlin'."

"You don't believe me? You think I secretly like to be referred to in such patronizing terms?"

"They're not patronizing, Stefanie. They're affectionate."

She frowned, realizing how petty she was being. And once again, she found herself hating to hear him use her proper name. So T.J. was right about her. She did like babe, and baby, and darlin', and whatever other endearments he came up with. "Sorry. I'm a bit edgy, I guess," she mumbled.

"Why, Steffie?"

She stared at him, realizing what she'd gotten herself into. She couldn't tell him she was edgy over his apparent lack of interest in being with her outside of work. She couldn't demand to know why he wasn't pushing for the reconciliation he'd claimed to want. She couldn't admit that her nights were lonelier than ever, thanks to the stimulation of the days spent with him. "Let's just get back to work," she said, giving up on trying to make excuses. She went to a teak cabinet and pulled out a plastic tube, taking the boat diagrams from it.

T.J. studied Stefanie as she smoothed the large sheets of paper out on her desk and put weights on the corners. He had his own theory about her increasing tension and hoped he wasn't deluding himself. "Sure, babe," he said pleasantly. "Work's what I'm here for, right?"

When Saturday arrived and T.J. was facing the prospect of two days without seeing Stefanie, he decided his self-discipline had its limits. "How about a movie tonight?" he suggested when he phoned her in the afternoon.

Stefanie firmly made up her mind to refuse. "What movie?"

"There are several in town I'd like to see, so you choose what appeals to you. Maybe we could grab something to eat first. Why don't I pick you up around six?"

Turn him down, Stefanie ordered herself. "Six would be fine," she heard herself saying. "But I can fix something for us here. A gumbo, maybe."

"You don't have to twist my arm for one of your gumbos, babe." T.J. was amazed that Stefanie would go so far as to fix his favorite food. His one concern was how he would keep his hands off her, but after a moment of wavering, he reminded himself yet again that merely seducing Stefanie wasn't his plan. He had to lay a foundation of friendship and trust before allowing passion to have its way. He didn't want Stefanie for a night. He wanted her for a lifetime.

On Sunday morning, when Stefanie woke up alone, she went back over the events of the previous night.

It had been a perfect evening, she mused as she stared up at the ceiling with a scowl. T.J. had raved about the gumbo, they'd talked and laughed easily together, the movie had been funny and romantic— and then he'd kissed her good night and left her.

In a way, she was glad. Much as she wanted him, she was aware that lovemaking would lead to the question of whether he should move in with her again, and she wasn't ready to give that situation another try. The pain would be too terrible if the experiment ended in failure.

Yet it drove her crazy that he was in such full control, while she knew she couldn't have resisted him if he'd suggested making love.

T.J. was stiff and sore in every part of his body when he showed up at the *Bayou Belle* on Monday afternoon for his orientation cruise.

He'd spent all of Sunday jogging, working out, swimming, and playing raquetball. He'd considered calling Stefanie during the afternoon to suggest going for a drive but hadn't dared. The Saturday night with her had tested his self-discipline to its limits.

Nevertheless, he was looking forward to the challenge of being a competent "professional gambler," an entertainer really. T.J. had dressed as Stefanie had instructed for his first day, in jeans and a red polo shirt, like an ordinary tourist.

As Stefanie joined him to board the riverboat, T.J.

smiled. She was as elegantly turned out as usual in a white linen pantsuit and hot pink silk shirt, her blond hair shining in the bright sunlight.

T.J. adored and admired his wife, not only for her loveliness, but for her brains, her imagination, her sheer stamina and determination. He knew how she'd armed herself with a business degree, then started on the very bottom rung in a tour company to learn all the ropes and make vital contacts. With a shrewd eye for investments, she'd parlayed a small inheritance from her grandmother into a respectable nest egg that she'd used to buy out a faltering riverboat company. After selling off all but one paddle wheeler, she'd refurbished it elegantly with polished mahogany, beveled glass, and gleaming brass fittings, and had added refreshment stands and classy souvenir concessions. She offered an unusually entertaining cruise at a healthy ticket price and had turned a profit after only a year. Even her idea of adding a gambling area for the sake of atmosphere and donating its profits to charity had enhanced her operation's reputation. Passengers who wanted to try their hand against a Hollywood-style gambler could enjoy themselves and feel good whether they won or lost.

And on top of her own achievement, Stefanie had come up with a plan to lead her younger sisters to success with Dreamweavers, Inc.

T.J. stood beside her at the railing of the top deck, watching the passengers arrive, listening to the lively Dixieland band—Stefanie had no compunction about mixing historical time periods to liven up the party, T.J. thought with amusement. As he caught the excitement in the air, he found it hard to remember that one of the people boarding the paddle wheeler could be a Gardner hireling

Wondering how far the man would go with his vendetta against Stefanie, T.J. decided to do a bit of checking on his own. Forewarned was forearmed; T.J. had learned that lesson the hard way. By underestimating how far an enemy of his would go to discredit him, he'd allowed himself to be set up for the tuna boat mess that had been so disastrous to his already shaky marriage. This time he was going to be smarter.

Eight

"For today, we'll just enjoy the cruise," Stefanie said, jarring T.J. from his thoughts.

He smiled. "Don't forget, I took the trip with you just after we met, so I'm not totally unfamiliar with the operation."

"But that was an evening dinner cruise," Stefanie said, fondly remembering the night she'd learned just how romantic her own paddle wheeler trip on the Mississippi could be, every line of the ship bordered by lights, the jazz soft and mellow.

She gave herself a little mental shake and went on. "We don't have gambling during the dinner cruises. And there are seldom many children. It makes a difference. Besides, that night you weren't studying the operation."

"No, babe, I wasn't," T.J. agreed with a tender smile.

Stefanie cleared her throat. "Well, this time, watch how our people stay on top of things, making sure the passengers have a good time, keeping an eye on their safety—especially the children. Every crew member, including the gambler when he's not playing cards in the casino, keeps an eye on the kids and tries to keep them out of trouble and entertained. And we never scold. We distract."

"Sounds like good parenting techniques, Steffie," T.J. said. "But then, I always did think you'd be a great mother."

She forced herself to ignore the suggestion implicit in his comment, and the inner stirrings it aroused. "Later, we'll go up to the casino and watch the action. . . ."

As Stefanie went on, it became increasingly difficult for T.J. to dredge up enthusiasm for the job he'd taken on. Perhaps he should have skipped the stupid games, he thought. It was still tempting to toss his wife over his shoulder and carry her off to some remote spot to make love to her until she admitted she couldn't live without him.

And as far as Gardner was concerned, T.J. didn't like the idea of waiting for the man to make his move. There had to be a better way to find out whether the threats were empty talk or a genuine problem.

But T.J. had decided to play things Stefanie's way, if only to prove he could. Besides, he did believe he was taking the right tack with her.

But it was difficult.

By Wednesday, T.J. was back in costume, and to his delight so was Stefanie, giving that day's passengers a special treat. She carried herself like a queen, wearing a blue satin gown with a full, sweeping skirt, low neckline, and black lace trim, her hair swept up and held in place with what looked like a diamond-studded comb. She even carried a fan and used it with all the coquetry of a true southern belle.

When she played a few hands of poker, she won more in an hour for the charities the operation supported than the regular gambler had taken in during three two-and-one-half-hour cruises, partly because of her playing ability, partly because men flocked to her table and were so besotted with her, they paid little attention to their cards.

T.J.'s ability to curb his jealous streak was sorely tested as he stood back in the ornately decorated salon and watched her performance. Yet he was captivated by a side of Stefanie he'd never seen before. For a few strange moments, she *became* a lady of questionable virtue who followed her own rules, who flouted conventional society by outplaying men at their own game, who laughed throatily and knew how desirable she was.

She took a break and suggested that T.J. sit in on a few hands. The nights spent pretending to be one of the bear poachers had helped more than he'd realized, T.J. thought as he assumed the identity of a long-time gambler. After that tense experience, anything else seemed easy.

On Friday, he was asked to handle an afternoon cruise on his own. The other gambler had been given the day off, but Stefanie appeared in costume, taking on the role of T.J.'s companion.

He earned a respectable sum for their charities, enjoyed the flattering and surprisingly bold attentions of a young lady or two, and noticed happily that Stefanie was sticking especially close to him.

He and Stefanie stood at the railing as the paddle wheeler headed back to the wharf, the passengers laughing and chattering and tapping their feet to the music of the *Bayou Belle*'s Dixieland band.

"You give 'em a good show, babe," T.J. said, slipping his arm around Stefanie's waist. "The red satin curtains on the windows of the salon, the banjo pickers, the tall tales spun by the Mark Twain types, the painless history lessons—your passengers get more than their money's worth. And even the ones who gamble and lose are happy because they know they've helped a worthy cause. You're a brilliant woman, Steffie. I always knew it, but I don't think I fully appreciated how brilliant until now."

Stefanie gazed at T.J., proud and happy and grateful. "You're the one who gave those people a good show today," she told him. "You not only had the gamblers feeling as if they were matching wits with a seasoned card handler—and taking it with good humor when you bested them—you charmed all the passengers. What's more, you did everything within the strict guidelines we have to follow. You're the best, T.J. I'm not just saying it, and I'm not being prejudiced." She laughed softly. "I almost wish I hadn't interviewed a reasonably promising replacement yesterday morning. I won't want to let him out of the wings even if I get to the point of believing he can be trusted."

"You'd better," he said, trying to cover how much it meant to him to have pleased her. "I can't take the pressure of being charming day in, day out for too long. But how will you know you can trust this character?"

"I'm checking his references very carefully. There's not much more I can do. And I'm hoping Gardner will make his move, if he's going to make one, while you're still on the job." She laughed. "Isn't that nice of me?"

"Oh, right. You're a real sweetheart," T.J. said, glowing inside at the compliment of her continuing faith in him.

Suddenly aware of how much T.J. was going through for her sake, Stefanie spoke softly. "Thank you, Johnny. Thank you so much. Even without the complication of worrying about what Gardner might do, I honestly don't know how I'd have managed if you hadn't pitched in to help. And I mean it when I say you're fantastic. I wouldn't ask you to keep on with a job that would drive you crazy, but I'm glad I've had the chance to see you in action."

T.J. decided his moment had arrived. Reaching into his vest pocket he pulled out one poker chip, took Stefanie's hand, pressed the chip into her palm, and curled her fingers back over it.

She stared at him for a moment, her heart beating out of control, her breathing almost stopped. "You're calling in one of the chips now?"

"That's right, babe."

She swallowed hard, feeling a flush steal over her throat as unbidden excitement mounted within her. "Okay. What is it worth?"

"Dinner."

"Dinner?"

"That's all. You go to dinner with me. Tonight. I'll pick you up around eight."

"You're not asking whether tonight at eight is convenient," she protested feebly.

"Do I have to, babe? I have your marker, remember?"

She nodded. With or without the marker, she couldn't resist his invitation. He heated her blood until she was robbed of common sense. "Eight, then."

He bent to brush a tantalizing kiss over her lips. "Dress down, babe. Not up."

She smiled and nodded. It was six o'clock. She had two hours. She would need every second in order to make herself look just right for T.J., yet two hours had never seemed longer.

•   •   •

"It's unlocked," T.J. heard Stefanie call after he'd knocked on the apartment door.

Frowning, he let himself in. Her door shouldn't be unlocked, he thought with concern.

"Sorry I'm running behind," Stefanie said from the bedroom. "I had a couple of phone calls when I got home. I won't be long. Help yourself to a drink; you know where everything is."

"You worry me, Steffie," he said as he moved slowly through the living room, reacquainting himself with what had been his home—the only place he'd thought of as home, at least since childhood. As a bachelor, he'd had a pleasant enough apartment, but not until he and Stefanie had put together their nest had he felt a sense of permanence, of belonging. "How do you know I'm not your neighborhood ax murderer?" he scolded absently.

She laughed. "I buzzed down to the lobby to let you into the building not two minutes ago, remember? That's when I unlocked this door."

Memories rushed in on T.J. with overwhelming force as every detail of the room brought back a moment of happiness he and Stefanie had shared.

The plants they'd nurtured from mere cuttings were thriving, some even blooming. The overstuffed, natural cotton couch and chairs they'd picked out during one quick furniture store visit were as inviting as ever. The flea-market oak tables he had refinished so proudly still gleamed like satin.

His glance went to the multicolored dhurrie rug that brought back memories of the Saturday morning when he and Stefanie had made up their minds to shop until they'd picked up every last accessory they would need. The minute they'd found the rug, they'd both liked it so much, they'd used it as an excuse to celebrate over café au lait and *beignets* at the Café du Monde. After a struggle to stuff the carpet into the car, then get it into the apartment, they'd given in to the temptation to initiate their new purchase in their own special way, and their shopping had been over for another week.

They never had finished putting the place together, and as T.J. realized Stefanie hadn't added a single touch since he'd left, he felt a lump forming in his throat. "You haven't made any changes to the old homestead," he murmured when she came out of the bedroom to join him. "There still isn't a lamp behind the couch," he added with a strained smile. "Or a print on that far wall."

Stefanie didn't know what to say. She hadn't given another thought to buying a print, and even though living without that needed lamp was inconvenient, she'd been reluctant to buy one. There had been no pleasure in decorating the apartment without T.J. there to share it.

T.J. focused his attention on Stefanie as she stood fastening a pair of chunky gold earrings he'd given her on their only Christmas together. He smiled. "I see your idea of dressing down hasn't changed, babe. You pull your hair back into a ponytail, wear designer slacks instead of a designer dress, and figure you're into your grubs."

Stefanie laughed, giving a dismissive shrug, though she'd settled on every detail of the outfit only after a great deal of thought about what would please T.J. "Somehow I didn't think my real grubs suited the occasion. These clothes will fit in anywhere, won't they?"

"Anywhere," T.J. said, taking time to enjoy a slow,

appreciative perusal of the throwaway elegance that was Stefanie's trademark: ivory linen slacks, a silk shirt the color of toffee, a lightweight paisley shawl draped over one shoulder and tucked into the narrow gold belt that circled her slender waist, beige Italian pumps. "You look like pralines and cream, babe," he murmured, moving close to her and resting his hands on her waist. "Mind if I steal a sample? I always did like having my dessert before the main course."

Before Stefanie could protest—though she hadn't planned to—she was tasting the minty sweetness of T.J.'s mouth and instantly craving more, her arms twining around his neck, her body responding to his warm strength with an eagerness she couldn't suppress. The kiss ended too soon; T.J. raised his head and smiled regretfully. "We always did have the problem of never getting to the main course when we'd had dessert first, didn't we, babe?"

Stefanie nodded, feeling as giddy and breathless as a teenager on her first important date. She kept her hands clasped at the nape of his neck and tipped back her head, smiling up at T.J., wondering how he managed to seem more handsome every time she saw him. In jeans, an open-collared blue shirt, and a black leather windbreaker, he exuded an aura of hard masculinity that made her forget everything but wanting him. "So what's planned for our main course?" she asked huskily.

T.J. gazed at her for several moments before making a difficult decision. "Well, I know what I'd like it to be, darlin', but I did have this little restaurant in mind . . ."

"Don't tell me," Stefanie said with a teasing grin, glad T.J. was strong enough for both of them. It seemed that every time he touched her, she wanted to invite him into her bed. "You've discovered another of your obscure mom-and-pop bistros in the French Quarter, the decor simple, the food out of this world, the wine cellar possibly the best in town."

T.J. laughed. "As a matter of fact, yes. But would you prefer something fancier? A big-name place? I could change my clothes—"

"Heavens no. I get enough of the big-name places when I'm squiring clients and political heavies, as you well know. I love these incredible finds of yours."

Pleased by Stefanie's receptiveness but almost wary, T.J. searched the smoky depths of her eyes.

Stefanie was mesmerized by T.J.'s penetrating green eyes. His effect on her was uncanny. She simply couldn't resist the man. He stripped her of her will, her sense, her strength. Yet she remembered moments when loving T.J. had given her a heady sense of boundless power and limitless horizons, and she'd begun to think those moments were worth all the pain.

"Where did you go?" T.J. asked.

Startled back to reality, Stefanie gave him a shaky smile. "The same place you did, I think."

He sighed deeply, struggling to keep his intense feelings in check. "A lot of heavy emotions are floating around in this apartment, babe. Maybe we'd better get out of here."

She nodded, moved out of the circle of his arms, and picked up her purse. "Maybe we'd better."

T.J. reached up and playfully tugged on her hair. "By the way, I like the ponytail."

He always had liked her hair that way, Stefanie thought with a contented grin.

As T.J. grasped the doorknob, he paused, unable

to leave the apartment without another look around. "When I came back the day after our quarrel to pick up some things—you were at work—I almost stayed," he heard himself saying in a voice barely loud enough to discern. "I came so close, Steffie. I wanted to stay. Why didn't I?"

"I'd hurt you too much," Stefanie answered with unflinching honesty. Along with her private, determined efforts to conquer her fear of storms, she'd been doing a lot of thinking, and she'd started facing some difficult truths. "T.J., let's both admit I let you down badly. And you didn't deserve it. I still can't sort out what was going on in my head, or what's going on there now, so I can't be sure I won't hurt you again." She paused, took a deep breath, then blurted out the rest of what she felt must be said. "Why would you want to take another chance on me?"

He stared at her as if she'd asked the strangest question of the century. "Because I love you, babe."

Just as Stefanie had predicted, T.J. took her to an out-of-the-way place she'd never heard of, a tiny room presided over by a small, bald Frenchman with a twitching Hercule Poirot mustache, constantly gesticulating hands, and an overflowing pride in the offerings of his wife's kitchen.

"You're a genius," Stefanie said lightly to T.J. as she finished the last of her crawfish creole. "How do you find these little gems? You could do a restaurant column and become a big hit just on the strength of your nose for great cooking." Still reeling from T.J.'s simple but heart-stopping words, *Because I love you, babe,* she'd been chattering like a magpie all evening.

"I would consider a restaurant column," T.J. said quite seriously.

Stefanie was taken aback. "You would?"

He nodded. "I wasn't kidding when I told you I was thinking of settling down, perhaps branching out into different kinds of feature writing. I think I'm slightly burned out on the environmental issues, at least from an exposé-writing standpoint. Maybe it's time for me to take on more upbeat topics. Besides, I want to stay close to home for a while." He grinned, a glint of fun appearing in his expressive eyes. "My wife needs me, you see."

"Oh, does she, now?"

"Definitely, though I'm not sure she realizes it."

Stefanie took a sip of her white wine. "And just what does she need you for, Mr. Carriere?"

T.J. chuckled quietly. "Do you really want to give me an opening like that?"

Stefanie gazed at him for a moment without saying a word, then nodded. "Yes, T.J., I do want to give you an opening like that."

"I'd forgotten how direct you can be," he said with a little shake of his head. "Well, let's see. Perhaps I should start by mentioning that the reasons my wife needs me are, by a strange coincidence, the very reasons I need her. For instance, there's the obvious," he said carefully, reaching across the table to take her hand in his, his thumb gently massaging her upturned palm. "We're pretty much dynamite in bed, you and I."

"Pretty much," Stefanie agreed, her voice soft with the desire T.J. could arouse in her so quickly, so easily.

"And think of the laughs we have together, babe."

"I think of them a lot," Stefanie said. "I don't laugh with anyone the way I do with you."

He felt hope and anticipation growing inside him. "And there's the dancing," he said, wondering why he would choose something so frivolous when the real reasons he believed he and Stefanie belonged together went so much deeper, so far beyond anything tangible.

Stefanie nodded. "I haven't danced in a long time. I miss it."

Elation was bubbling up inside T.J. like champagne. "How about tonight? I know where the Cajun music is the best in Louisiana."

"I thought you'd never ask," Stefanie said with a grin.

"We can have dessert and coffee there," T.J. said, signaling for the check, then smiling happily at Stefanie. "Between dances."

"I thought we already had dessert," she reminded him in a lazy drawl. "We started with it, remember?"

His gaze darkened as he brought her fingertips to his lips. "But you know how I am about dessert, darlin'. I never can get enough."

When the bill was paid, T.J. guided Stefanie outside, then couldn't contain his joy at the way the evening was going. He took Stefanie in his arms, hummed an old Cajun waltz, and whirled her around the base of a street lamp as if it were a crystal centerpiece at a grand cotillion.

Stefanie felt silly and carefree and exhilarated, heedless of the small audience she and T.J. were drawing, not even embarrassed when he made a sweeping bow to acknowledge a spontaneous burst of applause. "How had I managed to forget what a madman you are?" she asked, laughing as he tucked her in close to his body while they walked along the azalea-lined streets to his car.

"So had I, babe," he said, his lips close to her ear, his warm breath caressing her skin. "I think maybe you're the cause and the inspiration."

Stefanie wasn't surprised that the place T.J. had chosen for their dancing was a barn of a room with neon lights flashing behind the bar, foaming jugs of beer on the tables, and a live band that sounded as if it usually played on someone's back porch. "Only you, T.J.," she said with a delighted laugh, her whole body responding to the timeless rhythms even as she sat with him in a corner booth drinking a beer. "Only you ever brought me to a place like this."

T.J. laughed and squired her onto the floor, leading her through the uninhibited moves he'd taught her the first time they'd gone dancing together. "I saw through you from the beginning, babe," he said with a grin. "Under that elegant, dinner-at-Antoine's surface of yours is a down-home gal who likes an old-fashioned good time."

"You were right," she admitted, without reservation, then wound her arms around his neck, losing herself in heady pleasure as T.J.'s hands slid to her hips to move them in a swaying motion exactly paralleling his own. His intense gaze captured and held hers, his mouth hovered close to her mouth, his hard, muscular leg brushed against and between her thighs.

The crackling tension between them became unbearable after a while, the air sultry. "It's so hot," Stefanie murmured, barely aware she was speaking.

T.J. didn't answer. He merely danced her toward the saloon-style doorway and out into the night, then stopped, kept one arm around her while he cupped her chin in his hand and smiled down at her. "Is it cooler now?" he asked softly.

Stefanie wagged her head slowly from side to side. "Hotter than ever."

The blood began thundering through T.J.'s veins. The invitation in Stefanie's heavy-lidded eyes, her swollen lips, her low, husky voice was unmistakable. "Where could we go to cool off, babe?"

"How about your place?" Stefanie heard herself suggest, as if some mindlessly sensual part of her had taken full control.

T.J. tried to tell himself he was straying from his well-thought-out campaign to get the two of them back together permanently, but his hunger for Stefanie was too sharp to ignore. "My place it is," he said in a hoarse whisper, putting his arm around his wife's shoulders, holding her close to his side, ignoring the reminders of his conscience to go slowly and carefully.

Nine

"Nice place," Stefanie murmured as she looked around the living room of T.J.'s apartment.

He hadn't given much thought to the impersonal furnishings that had come with the suite. "It's comfortable enough," he answered, suddenly as awkward with Stefanie as if they were strangers.

Stefanie, too, felt ill at ease; the ride in the car had served as a cooling-off period, her practical mind recalling all sorts of excellent reasons why she should go home by herself and lock herself in.

Turning to look at him, she tried to find a way to explain that she'd made a mistake, that she had to leave. But the words died in her throat. She *hadn't* made a mistake. If she'd have to pay tomorrow for a night of pleasure, she would pay willingly.

But she didn't want to leave T.J. with any illusions. "No guarantees?" she asked, her heart hammering against her chest. With an effort at a smile, she added, "Or, as you would say in your phony Cajun accent, no gar-awn-tees?"

A battle raged inside T.J. He wanted Stefanie, but he didn't like her ground rules. He put his hands on her waist to draw her close to him, then reached up to remove the covered elastic band holding her ponytail.

Stefanie closed her eyes, reveling in the delicious feeling of her hair tumbling to her shoulders, T.J.'s fingers combing through the strands with infinite gentleness. "You haven't answered me," she managed to say.

"What guarantees do you want to avoid?" he asked softly.

"Of where we go from here. We take tonight and . . ."

"And the devil take tomorrow?" T.J. said warily.

Stefanie opened her eyes to look at him. "I can't help wanting you, T.J., but . . . well, you want me, too, so why should we push for more?"

T.J. knew he'd changed from the man he'd been a few months ago when, instead of being hurt by Stefanie's determined resistance to commitment, he saw clearly what she needed from him. "Sure, babe," he said at last, grinning and scooping her up in his arms. "We want each other. It's enough. Enough for tonight, anyway."

Stefanie was delighted by T.J.'s Rhett Butler manner, but she wasn't sure what to make of his answer. "I'm trying to avoid misunderstandings, that's all," she said nervously. "I mean, why can't we keep what's good between us and . . . well, and . . ."

"And discard the rest?" T.J. said, pushing open the door to his bedroom. Depositing Stefanie on the bed, he kicked off his shoes and stretched out over her. "Why, of course, honey. I'm all for discarding anything that isn't good between us." His hand went to the buttons of her blouse. "Like this bit of silk, for instance. Not that it's bad, but it has served its purpose, so let's get rid of it."

Stefanie's eyes widened in feigned innocence. "Served its purpose? Are you suggesting something improper on my part, Mr. Carriere?"

"Improper? My Steffie? Never. She wouldn't wear a silk blouse with nothing under it deliberately, knowing how it drives me crazy, now would she?" As he undid the last button and pushed aside the cloth, he inhaled sharply. Somehow he hadn't prepared himself for the sight of Stefanie's rich firm breasts, the creamy ivory skin tipped with dusky rose. "I've missed these lovely breasts," he said softly, smoothing one palm over the sweet bounty that was his—at least for the moment. "I've missed everything about you, Steffie."

Bending his head, T.J. blazed a trail of hot kisses over her throat while he stroked her hair back from her face with one hand and gently kneaded one full globe with the other. Stefanie clasped her hands at the nape of his neck, closed her eyes, and felt as if she'd become the embodiment of pure, pleasurable sensation. Yet a tiny part of her mind struggled to stay in control. "You do understand, then? You won't start acting like a—a husband?"

T.J. chuckled, a sound of deep male satisfaction as he realized how hard Stefanie was fighting to rule her instincts and how quickly her instincts were taking over. "Act like a husband? Would I do that, baby?" he asked, nibbling at her lower lip, then moving his mouth over hers and delving his tongue into her hot, sweet cavern.

Stefanie's tongue dueled with T.J.'s, her nipples hardening as his fingers teased them. Her breathing became labored, her thoughts gradually losing co-herence.

"By the way," T.J. said when he released her mouth so they could catch their breath, "what does a hus-band act like?"

Stefanie opened her eyes and tried to give him a playfully disdainful look, but suspected she man-aged only to gaze adoringly at the rascal. "You know what I mean, T.J. Carriere."

"No, I don't babe. And I wouldn't want to make a mistake, so you have to help me a little. For in-stance, if I were acting like a husband, would I do this?" He bent to capture one of her nipples between his lips, then flicked his tongue over it until Stefanie was gasping with delight.

"I swear, you are the worst tease in all creation," Stefanie said when he stopped to smile down at her with a gleam of sensual mischief in his green eyes.

"The worst?" he asked, looking wounded. "I'll try harder." He brought her other nipple to eager atten-tion, at the same time moving his hand to Stefanie's belt to undo it.

"All right," she said shakily when he raised his head to admire his handiwork. "You're the *best* tease in all creation. Is that description more to your liking?"

"It's quite a billing to live up to, darlin', but let's see what I can do." Nibbling at her bottom lip while he undid the fastenings of her slacks, he sensed that he'd handled the difficult moment the right way, that Stefanie was happy he hadn't accepted her just-for-tonight rider, yet was glad not to fight about it. One thing hadn't changed about his wife: She had a way of constantly challenging and testing him, as if making sure she couldn't bend him to her will but trying nonetheless.

He understood Stefanie now. While she wanted him to be strong, part of her was afraid of his strength. So he had to reassure her. "I think it's time to discard a few more of the not-so-good things between us," he said, sliding one arm under Stefanie to lift her body and ease off her blouse. When he'd tossed it to a nearby chair, he stood and quickly stripped off his clothes, his gaze never leaving Stefanie's as she watched his every move.

"You're magnificent," she said, as she took in the wide shoulders and broad, hard chest, the inverted triangle of dark, springy hairs, the lean hips and powerful thighs, the evidence of his virility, which made her heart pound with anticipation.

Moved by Stefanie's soft expression, T.J. bent to kiss her again, waves of tenderness washing over him. "And now let's get rid of the rest of our problems," he said with a smile, moving to the foot of the bed. With his gaze still locked on hers, he took off Stefanie's shoes, reached up to pull off her slacks, and once more caught his breath when he saw that she'd worn ivory lace bikini panties and ivory thigh-high stockings with lace instead of the panty hose she knew he hated. "The lady didn't have seduction on her mind this evening, of course," he teased.

Stefanie merely smiled, saying nothing, not caring that T.J. knew how much she wanted him. She was lost, waiting eagerly to feel the heat and hardness of him against her.

Very slowly, deliberately, T.J. removed each of Stefanie's stockings, kissing every inch of shimmering, pale gold skin he bared, then tugged off the last wisp of lace. "As I said earlier this evening," he murmured, touching his lips to the insides of her thighs, his fingertips feathering over her stomach, "you're like pralines and cream. And this time, darlin', I'm going to take more than a sample."

Stefanie was startled. She hadn't expected T.J. to demand such special intimacy, such total surrender to him so soon, and she heard herself protesting softly. "Johnny, no, not yet . . . Johnny . . ." Her voice faded into a deep sigh as she gave in to the delights T.J. knew so well how to give her.

At last, after arousing her until she was crying out for fulfillment, he moved over her, his knees parting her thighs. "I'm afraid I'm about to act like a husband," he murmured, poising himself at the entrance to her moist warmth but holding back, playing a tantalizing game of love they'd played before, though never with the serious stakes he'd decided on for this match. "You're sure you want me to do this?"

Stefanie's eyes were glazed as she looked up at him. But she understood, and at that moment she loved him for his determination to coax a commitment from her. "What you are, T.J. Carriere, is the *cruelest* tease in all creation," she said fiercely, knowing she would succumb at last to whatever he wanted but enjoying the game too much to give in without a battle. Wrapping her arms and legs around him, she moved her hips and tried in vain to take what she wanted but succeeded only in arousing herself to the point of unbearable desire.

Suddenly, paroxysms of need gripped Stefanie. She couldn't hold out another second. "Then act like a husband, Johnny," she whispered. "Love me the way a husband loves his wife. Let me love you . . . the way a wife loves her husband."

T.J. exhaled slowly, realizing only then that he'd been holding his breath. Sliding his hands under her to cup her buttocks, he dug his fingers into her soft flesh, raised her to give him total access, then plunged into her.

"I do love you," he murmured as he paused, awed by the sheer beauty of the moment. "I love you, baby."

Stefanie's eyes filled with tears as she realized that at this moment, with her body enveloping T.J., her world was right and complete again for the first time in months. "And I love you, Johnny," she murmured.

"I know, babe." His arms tightened around her and he lifted her hips even higher as his thrusts deepened. "I know. You're all mine, Steffie. Don't ever forget it. I won't *let* you forget it. Now give me everything, sweetheart. You can't hold back, so don't try. Just know you're mine, and let go of everything else."

Stefanie moaned helplessly as T.J.'s mesmerizing voice and the power of his body left her no choice but to obey.

Suddenly, she felt as if she'd burst through some invisible barrier to soar high above the fear-ridden person she'd been. She was drugged with love and pleasure and need, and only T.J. could guide her through these strange new realms. "Johnny, don't let me get away from you," she cried, hardly aware of what she was saying. "Hold me, Johnny . . . Johnny . . ."

Her voice faded as T.J.'s movements drove out all semblance of thought, leaving only perfect ecstasy. Stefanie gazed into the infinite mystery of T.J.'s eyes as he carried her to a pinnacle higher than any she'd known before.

And T.J. looked into the soft, velvety gray of Stefanie's eyes, knowing that for this moment, this single poignant moment, she was truly his wife.

• • •

Stefanie didn't know how long she'd slept when she woke to find herself nestled, spoon style, against T.J., his hand carelessly cupping her breast. He was a cocoon of warmth around her, and she thought she should feel trapped. But she didn't. She felt secure. As desire washed over her again in a delicious wave, she rotated her hips a little.

Though he was asleep, T.J.'s response was immediate. His hand began kneading her soft breast while he pressed himself against her.

Within seconds, he was inside her again, his hands curved around her hips as if to hold her in place while he took his pleasure. But his pleasure was Stefanie's joy, his explosion the trigger for hers.

They fell asleep again, still joined, T.J.'s hand once again gently cupping Stefanie's breast.

The morning light broke the spell.

Stefanie opened her eyes to the sun's rays pouring through the open window, and was mortified by the shamelessness of her total surrender to T.J.

A burning flush spread over her body as she remembered the things she'd said to him during the night, the things she'd done. He'd stripped her of every inhibition, but more, he'd robbed her of her separate will.

Carefully, she started to get out of bed.

"Where are you off to, babe?" T.J. asked.

She jumped, instinctively grabbing the corner of the sheet to cover herself.

T.J. grinned and reached for her, pulling her into his arms. "A little panic setting in, darlin? You're remembering that you're supposed to be the cool, independent, strong Stefanie Sinclair, and you're wondering how to square her with the woman you became last night?"

"Passion has nothing to do with reality," Stefanie answered primly, struggling against the languid warmth beginning to pervade her body as T.J.'s strong arms cuddled her against him.

"Passion has everything to do with reality, Steffie. In fact, for you, passion is the only reality. You're passionate about everything in your life." He chuckled as he nuzzled her ear. "Even about trying to fight being so passionate."

"That kind of thinking is too convoluted for me, I'm afraid," Stefanie said, though she understood exactly what T.J. meant and suspected he was right.

"Any kind of thinking is a mistake right now," he murmured, tugging away the sheet she still clutched to cover herself. "Don't think, Steffie. Do what you did last night. Just feel."

Stefanie had no choice as T.J.'s hands and lips aroused her yet again. But even as T.J. pulled her on top of him, she tried to preserve a tiny grain of separateness. "There's an existence beyond what we feel here, T.J., an everyday, mundane reality beyond lovemaking that we never learned to deal with. Surely you remember . . ." Her protest was lost in her gasp of pleasure as T.J. lifted her body and lowered her onto him, impaling her so deeply she felt as if he'd penetrated her whole being.

"I remember," he said as he moved within her. "Even our battles were passionate. There was never any indifference, though. We couldn't deal with indifference. We can and will learn to deal with our clashing wills."

Stefanie tipped back her head as intense pleasure

racked her body. "T.J., you make it sound so easy. I wish I could believe you."

"It won't be easy," he said, his voice a soft rasp as excitement began to overtake him. "Just possible, babe. Now, let go again. Flow with me. Don't fight what's happening, darlin'. You can't win if you try to fight. You can win only when you stop fighting. And don't call me T.J. Call me Johnny. I love the sound of your voice when you say that name. Say it, baby. Say my name."

His voice was like a focal point for Stefanie in an abyss where there was nothing else for her to cling to. "Johnny," she whispered, grasping his strong, muscular arms for support. "Don't let me think, Johnny. I hate thinking. I just want to love you."

"Then love me, sweet baby," he said as his movements deepened and quickened. "Love me, trust me, give yourself to me. I won't let you down again. I'll always be there for you."

Tears spilled from Stefanie's eyes, rolled down her cheeks and splashed onto T.J.'s chest. "Don't ever leave me again," she begged. "Don't let me leave you."

"Not a chance, baby. I told you last night. You're all mine. You don't have a choice anymore. I'm keeping you forever. When those damned doubts of yours come creeping back, remember what I'm telling you, Steffie. You're my wife, and my wife you'll stay. Not like before. Everything's going to be different this time. Remember it, because I will." Then with a new, heady sense of power, T.J. gave his own passion full sway until he was pouring his love into Stefanie, awash in unimaginable rapture, praying his words would drive out all her doubts.

•   •   ••

"I think I hate you," Stefanie said without conviction hours later, when they were back in T.J.'s bed after the long, sensual shower they'd had together.

He hadn't let her leave or even get dressed—not that she'd tried very hard to do either. He'd brought food to the bedroom on trays to give them strength for what had turned out to be a marathon of pleasuring each other, as if they were trying to catch up on six months of loneliness in one weekend.

"You love me," T.J. said, pressing his lips to her forehead. "But why are you claiming to hate me?"

"You know why, dammit."

He crooked his finger under her chin and tilted up her face so he could grin down at her with a look of mock innocence. "I have no idea, babe."

"Because you're taking advantage of me."

"Wrong," T.J. said with a laugh. "It's because I couldn't and wouldn't make you do anything you didn't want to do, including staying in this bed with me."

"We can't stay here forever," Stefanie said, pointedly ignoring the truth of what T.J. had said. "Once I'm out of here, I'll be my own person again."

T.J. chuckled quietly. "Sure, babe."

It had become a matter of pride, or at least of saving what shreds were left of her pride, for Stefanie to battle T.J. between bouts of lovemaking. Or perhaps it was part of their sensual sparring. Stefanie wasn't sure anymore. "I was out of my mind to let you seduce me last night. It's not as if I didn't know the dangers waiting for me if I lowered my guard."

"Let's keep the record straight, darlin'," T.J. said cheerfully. "You did the seducing, remember? You wore the silk blouse with no bra under it, the stockings instead of panty hose. You said you were hot—

and you were—and you wanted to come back here to make love. Which reminds me: Why this apartment? Why not our own?"

Stefanie didn't answer.

T.J. realized his quest was far from over. Stefanie was going to be stubborn, at this point simply because she couldn't cope with the knowledge of how completely she'd given herself to him. "You were afraid I'd decide to stay?" he asked. "By coming here, you held on to just that much control, knowing you could leave?"

"*Thinking* I could leave," she corrected him. "You've made it clear you don't plan to let me go anywhere. Besides, if you decide you want to move back into our apartment, you'll make love to me again and tease me until I'm begging you to start packing your suitcases. It's disgusting how you can make me say just about anything at certain . . . moments."

T.J. couldn't suppress a tiny smile. He'd noticed how Stefanie had followed his lead in referring to the apartment as theirs not hers. And he was just vain enough to be pleased by her admission that he could harness her passion to get what he wanted. "Baby, I wouldn't try to extract that kind of decision from you when I know your thinking processes are on hold. But thanks for saying I could."

She gave him a fierce look. "I *do* hate you."

He laughed contentedly. He was beginning to recognize when Stefanie meant what she was saying and when she was just talking to hear herself. "I'll move back into the apartment when I'm invited," he told her, then reached down and ran one finger along the length of her thigh. "Am I invited?"

Stefanie longed to have him come home, yet she panicked at the thought of it and still wasn't sure why. "No," she blurted almost desperately.

"Why not?"

"Because—because we'd fight."

"About what, darlin'?"

"You name it, we'd fight about it, just the way we used to."

"No, babe. *You* name it. You're the one who thinks we haven't learned anything."

Stefanie had to think hard to remember the causes of their battles. Nothing seemed worth mentioning.

"Stuck for an answer?" T.J. asked with a wicked grin.

Suddenly Stefanie had an important thought. "My work. You were at me constantly about being a workaholic. Yet you were just as bad. You didn't know how to turn down an assignment, even if you had to work around the clock to meet your deadlines."

"I admit it," T.J. said quietly. "I did take on too many assignments. It's a free-lancer's occupational hazard. When we start out, we discover that a journalist's life is feast or famine—too many assignments or not enough to pay the rent. I was just beginning to realize that I was established enough to pick and choose, when I suddenly found myself married to a highly successful woman, and I went into a whole new panic about making sure I wasn't riding on her coattails."

Stefanie twisted out of his arms, sat up, and stared down at him. "You're joking!"

"It's not the kind of thing I joke about, babe. I was running scared in my own way. It took losing you to make me see that it's not important for me to chase every dollar and every bit of recognition that comes my way."

"Are you saying my success threatened you?" Stefanie asked, still unable to absorb this unexpected bit of information. "Is that why you nagged me about working so much?"

T.J. was tempted to say it was, but he knew that honesty was essential to making a permanent peace with Stefanie. "No, darlin'. I was and am proud of your success. I understand that your business requires a big commitment from you. I nagged you about working so hard because you used your career as a way to even some mythical score between us. If I had no time for us because of my work, you managed to have no time for us because of yours. Your business became a shield to keep me from getting what looked to you to be the upper hand. And Dreamweavers was a handy little haven, a place to go when you were afraid I was getting too close to you. You're scared of me, Steffie."

Stefanie sat back against the headboard and absently pulled a sheet up over her breasts. "Nonsense. Honestly, I think I should call you T.J. Freud and buy you a couch. Why would I be afraid of you?" she muttered, though she couldn't suppress the memory of the day her mother had accused her of being terrified of her husband.

T.J. grinned and let her protect herself with the sheet for the moment. "You're used to being in charge, babe. You've been used to it since you were a little girl keeping your sisters in line. People are very much in awe of you, from your family to your employees. You're a terrific controller. The best. You're pleasant, thoughtful, giving, generous, fair. But you're convinced you're top dog, so everyone falls obediently into line. But I've seen glimpses of the soft, vulnerable Steffie who gets a little tired of being Superwoman, who might like to relax and let someone else take over occasionally. The trouble is *that* Steffie is afraid if she lets go of the reins even for a while, she'll never get them back."

Stefanie felt her insides tighten into a knot. T.J. really did have her number. She'd never felt so vulnerable.

Yet was his understanding so terrible? Did she still have so little trust in him that she would destroy the happiness they could have together rather than let him know her, with all her fears and faults?

Suddenly she dropped the sheet she'd been clutching and leaned over T.J., brushing her breasts over his hard, hair-roughened chest, bending her head so her hair caressed his skin.

"Time to stop thinking again?" T.J. asked softly.

Stefanie closed her lips over one hard nipple, exulting in its sensitivity, realizing she had a power of her own over T.J. But did it match his over her? She couldn't exist in an unequal relationship, yet she loved a man who was the epitome of male strength, in his own charming way.

T.J. reached for Stefanie, planning to take her in his arms and love her again.

She pushed his hands away and gave him a smile of pure, feminine challenge. "It's my turn, Johnny. Let's see whether I can drive you as wild as you drive me."

T.J.'s heart beat faster with excitement. There was no doubt in his mind what Stefanie could do to him. "Please be gentle," he said with a mischievous, loving smile.

Much, much later it occurred to him that the bedroom wasn't a bad place for working out the constant power struggle between himself and his wife. As they lay together in exhausted bliss, he sensed that Stefanie was beginning to accept the seesaw of dominance that would be their style for the rest of their lives. "Fifty-fifty," she'd said so often during their brief marriage. "Total equality in all things," she'd demanded, adding as an ideal, "with peace, harmony, and quiet affection. I hate these storms of ours."

Storms, T.J. thought, wondering whether she could ever conquer her deep fear of all kinds of storms.

The ideal marriage she'd described had been the one she'd seen between her parents, never realizing that such a placid relationship would bore her to tears.

He supposed it wasn't feasible to keep Stefanie in bed for the next fifty years.

But knowing how she would start bracing herself for trouble when the weekend of unalloyed joy, of mindless pleasure, was over, he was sorely tempted to give it a try.

Ten

T.J. was frustrated.

It had been nearly two weeks since the blissful weekend with Stefanie, and he felt as if he were losing ground rather than gaining it.

Just as he'd anticipated, their return to reality had brought back her conviction that love and marriage, contrary to the old song, didn't go together like a horse and carriage—unless she were holding the reins.

She'd reverted to her old habit of hiding behind her work, and though she was legitimately busy with Dreamweavers, she also used the demands of her company as a way to keep T.J. at arms' length, to take control of the situation, rationing out their times together as if their renewed closeness was a forbidden treat not a vibrant reality of her whole existence. And she somehow managed to make sure they didn't make love in her bed—the bed that once had been theirs.

He'd begun to fear he'd done irreparable harm to

his cause by making love to Stefanie, reminding her how vulnerable she was to him. Understanding her withdrawal, T.J. still found it hard to take. What was worse, he kept questioning his own response, wondering if he should be more aggressive and simply not allow Stefanie to take over. Perhaps she was testing him, hoping . . . Yet on the other hand, perhaps . . .

Cut it out! he told himself as he unlocked his apartment door after his ninth successful and uneventful afternoon cruise on the *Bayou Belle*. The constant internal arguments about the best way to handle Stefanie were getting to him, and if he wasn't careful, his concentration during card games would start faltering—a potential disaster.

After some nosing around about Stuart Gardner and his chemical company, T.J. was convinced that the man would try to strike out at Stefanie in some way. But T.J. had decided not to let anything happen to Stefanie or her company, and he'd already begun his own private campaign to protect her.

Since he'd cut his journalistic teeth as a newspaper reporter in New Orleans, and still had a lot of friends in the local media, he'd put out a few feelers and was calling in some markers. If Stuart Gardner was up to anything that would involve bad publicity for Dreamweavers, T.J. was confident of knowing what the man was up to before any damage could be done.

As he tossed his hat onto the closet shelf, T.J. noticed that the message light on his answering machine was on.

Maybe Stefanie had called, he thought with a surge of hope. He hadn't seen her for a couple of nights, and he missed her. Perhaps she missed him too.

The first message was from Ken Harmer, a syndicated columnist who'd been given his first break as a reporter on the strength of T.J.'s recommendation. "I have some information for you," Ken's no-nonsense voice said. "Give me a call so we can arrange to get together."

Certain that Ken's information must be important, T.J. phoned back immediately. He reached Ken's answering machine and said he'd try again later. Disappointed and curious, he absently hit the playback button once more and was taken aback to hear Stefanie's low, lovely voice. "Hi, Johnny. I just thought I'd find out how things have been going on the *Bayou Belle.* Sorry I've been out of touch for a couple of days—I've been swamped at work. I'm home for the evening if you feel like giving me a call."

T.J. played the message three times, trying to decide what Stefanie had really wanted to say. She sounded terribly tired and, unless he was imagining things, a bit wistful.

He was about to call her and go through the usual game of trying to find out whether she wanted to see him, when he abruptly made a decision. He'd been pussy-footing around long enough. It was time to take action. He knew his wife. It was time for him to take advantage of that knowledge.

After a quick change to jeans, sneakers, and a white sweatshirt, he headed for her place—with one stop on the way.

Stefanie frowned when the apartment intercom buzzed. Her frown turned to a tiny grin when she heard T.J.'s voice. And she beamed when she opened the door to find him standing there with a large, insulated bag from her favorite oriental restaurant.

"You always did have an uncanny knack for knowing when I was too tired for anything more energetic than Chinese food right from the cartons," she said, her whole body suddenly infused with new energy, charged with the excitement of seeing T.J. unexpectedly.

She had stood back and welcomed T.J. with an affectionate kiss on the cheek before she remembered that she hadn't planned for him to spend an evening alone with her in the apartment. It was too much like old times, too reminiscent of their married life. She wasn't ready to resume living with T.J., much as she longed to be with him all the time.

"I got your message, babe," T.J. said, putting the food on the large square coffee table in the middle of the living room. "You sounded beat. And you look worn out. What've you been doing to yourself?"

"Bahamian bureaucrats," she answered, her frown returning as she glanced down at her red shorts and white T-shirt, her hand going to her hair, which was carelessly pulled back with a plain silver barrette at the nape of her neck.

T.J. grinned and hauled her into his arms. "I said you look worn out, darlin'. But you're still the prettiest girl I know."

"I'm a mess," she grumbled, at the same time nestling happily into the warmth of T.J.'s body and touching her lips to the sweetly familiar hollow of his throat. "I wasn't expecting company."

"Am I still considered company here?" he asked quietly.

Stefanie tilted back her head to look up at him. "In the sense that I prefer to look nice for you, you're company."

He chuckled. "Spoken like a real diplomat. But you look terrific, and if you don't know that you look terrific, the man in your life hasn't been showering you with enough compliments. Shall I begin? Let's talk about your gorgeous legs for starters. Long and tanned and shapely—"

"The man in my life showers me with plenty of compliments," Stefanie interrupted, feeling oddly shy. "Also with Chinese food, which is getting cold." She gave T.J. a quick hug, then moved away to drop to a cross-legged sitting position beside the coffee table. "The man in my life is also very thoughtful," she added as she started taking cartons from the bag and opening them.

"Certain traditions have to be upheld, especially the one that says I buy Chinese food for my lady when she's tired." T.J. sat beside Stefanie and opened two cellophane packets of chopsticks, then checked the cartons until he found the one he wanted first. "Here are the egg rolls, babe. And the plum sauce. What's this about Bahamian bureaucrats, by the way?"

Stefanie took an egg roll, squeezed sauce onto it, and ate a bit before answering. "I'm helping Morgan get the red tape out of the way for her expansion into Nassau. I invited a couple of visiting Bahamian officials to check out our operation. I took them on the Lake Pontchartrain pirate ship this afternoon and the *Bayou Belle* dinner cruise last night, went over Morgan's marketing reports with them, and generally wined and dined and quizzed them. It's best to know the potential pitfalls in advance." Stefanie grinned. "As my wise husband used to say to me, forewarned is forearmed."

T.J. didn't trust his own ears. Had Stefanie called

him her husband? He let the moment pass because he feared she'd take back her words if he asked her to repeat them. Instead, he conceded an old sore point between them. "I know I've always said you could do more delegating, babe, and I still think so, but it's obvious there are chores only you can look after." He tried a dumpling, nodded approvingly, dipped his chopsticks into the carton to snag another, and held it out to Stefanie. "I think maybe you were right when we used to fight about your work. You said I didn't understand the demands of the company."

Stefanie ate the dumpling, then smiled, thinking how odd it was that T.J. was beginning to see her side of things just when she'd started to see his. "It's also possible that I *could* delegate more in certain areas. For instance, I have to make a presentation to a jazz club tomorrow night. Its members are interested in getting Lisa to organize southern France tours to coincide with the Nice jazz festival in July. Obviously Lisa can't be here to make the pitch, but if I'd taken your advice and hired a good marketing person, I wouldn't have to do it. It's time I started to pick and choose my chores, just as you've begun to pick and choose your writing assignments. You know something, Johnny? I'm tired of being tired."

Again, T.J. wasn't sure what to make of her remarks. Was she telling him that some of their differences might be resolved with a little give and take on both sides?

They were both quiet as they finished eating, their usual easy camaraderie stilted by their acute awareness of being together in the home they'd shared, sitting on the floor and eating Chinese food from cartons as they'd done so often.

"I gather nothing unusual has happened on the *Bayou Belle*," Stefanie said, almost startling T.J. as she broke into his thoughts.

"Not yet," he answered, putting down his chopsticks.

Stefanie started gathering the debris and putting it into the original bag. "You sound as if you think it's just a matter of time until Gardner makes his move."

"Let's just say I intend to be ready for him."

Stefanie smiled again, glad T.J. was on her side. He could be a formidable opponent. "I'm hearing great things from the *Bayou Belle*'s recreation director and other people on the crew about you," she said after a pause.

T.J. raised one brow. "Are you checking up on me, darlin'?"

"Of course not, silly. The comments were unsolicited. I also hear you're terribly popular with our lady passengers."

He raised two brows. "A touch of jealousy? From a lady who thinks possessiveness is practically a crime?"

"I'm not jealous," Stefanie answered. "I'm merely mentioning that I've heard how the ladies are falling all over you, how sweet young things are throwing themselves at you quite shamelessly."

"But you're not jealous," T.J. said, his lips twitching with humor.

"Not a bit." Stefanie suddenly burst out laughing. "All right, you win. My eyes are greener than yours, if you must know. But I still say that jealousy is a childish emotion, and I intend to overcome it. So there."

"Well, good for you, babe. I'm trying to overcome it myself. Maybe we can help each other. The buddy system, so to speak."

"Like the one we're using to deal with Stuart Gardner," Stefanie said, her thoughts returning to how much T.J. was going through to help her fight her battle. She knew he couldn't be enjoying his job on the riverboat, yet he was doing it for her sake. "Johnny, how do I keep thanking you for so many things without sounding gushy? I can't begin to express how much it means to me to know you're around to handle whatever Gardner might try. I'd be frantic with worry if you hadn't decided to help me out. As it is, I probably don't give the situation as much thought as I should."

T.J. couldn't help being encouraged. Stefanie seemed to be reaching out to him, trying to tell him that the problems keeping them apart were gradually dissolving. "You don't have to thank me," he said softly. "I love you, Steffie. To do something for you is to do it for myself. Even though we still have problems, in my mind we're a team. We're part of each other. Indivisible. You know that, don't you?"

"Oh, Johnny, I want us to be that way," Stefanie said in a husky plea. "What's holding me back? I love you more than ever, but to think of trying again . . ." As tears began spilling from her eyes, she jumped to her feet and searched in vain in her pockets for a tissue. "There isn't another soul in the world who can make me cry, but I seem to dissolve into stupid tears at the drop of a hat when I'm around you. And I never, never, never have a damned handkerchief! What's the matter with me, anyway?" Whirling, she raced to the bedroom for a box of tissues and a moment of privacy.

T.J. sat in stunned silence for several moments, then got up and followed Stefanie, hating the fact that he kept making her cry.

He stopped dead as he stepped into the bedroom. Stefanie was in front of the mirrored oak dresser, wiping her eyes. His silver-handled hairbrush was on the dresser, exactly where he'd left it, his leather tie-tack case beside it, along with a pewter-framed photograph of him.

With a quizzical glance at Stefanie, T.J. went to the closet where he'd left some of his clothes and opened it. Everything was still there, though now encased in plastic garment bags—a sign of Stefanie's typical efficiency.

He turned to her as he shut the closet door, his brows knitting in puzzlement. "It's as if I'd never been gone," he said quietly.

She shrugged, a little embarrassed. Wandering around in a daze since her return from Key West, she hadn't stopped to think that T.J. probably would see that she hadn't moved his belongings. "I thought I should take decent care of your things until you had a chance to pick them up," she said lamely.

T.J. kept staring at her in shock. Stefanie looked down at the floor, then at T.J. again. "Well, I *did* think I should take care of them. But—" She closed her eyes to say the rest, unable to face him while admitting her foolish sentimentality. "The truth is, I couldn't bring myself to move anything, change anything. I went into a strange kind of limbo when you left. I still functioned, but in a disjointed way, pretending I was intact when I wasn't. It was as if . . . as if . . ."

"As if half of you were missing?" he said gently.

She opened her eyes and gave him a tentative smile. "You too?"

"Me, too, babe. So why are we playing this cat-and-mouse game? Why aren't we together?"

Stefanie said nothing.

T.J. moved to her and curled his fingers around her shoulders. "Why, Steffie? What are you trying to prove? Are you punishing me?"

"Of course I'm not punishing you!"

"Then why haven't I moved back home, Steffie? Why do I live in one apartment, you in another? You've admitted you love me, you've shown it in countless ways, yet you're fighting our marriage with everything you've got. Why?"

Stefanie twisted out of his grasp and moved to stand with her back to him, saying nothing, her arms folded tightly over her chest.

T.J. reached into his pocket, pulled out a poker chip, and tossed it to the dresser. "It's my second chip, babe," he said quietly. "Honor your marker by giving me some answers."

Stefanie stared at the chip, then began slowly. "I went through hell when you left," she said, just above a whisper. "There was nothing in my life but a horrible emptiness, a cold that settled so deeply into my bones I felt as if I'd never be warm again. It didn't help to know that I'd driven you away. The pain was even worse because I deserved it. I don't want to go through it again. I survived, T.J., but I'm not sure I could manage a second time."

Standing behind Stefanie, T.J. reached out to her, then dropped his hands, knowing at last that he couldn't keep depending on physical closeness to break through the barrier she'd raised around herself. "Baby, why are you so sure there'll be a second time?"

She turned, her eyes dark with tears and wrenching emotion. "Because there was a *first* time! Because I believed we loved each other so much, nothing could come between us. Then, all of a sudden, you were gone. Just—just gone. I didn't know where. You said I didn't give you a chance to defend yourself, and it's true. I hate myself for the way I treated you. But you didn't give me much chance either. I fell short of your image of what a wife should be, loyal, trusting, and you didn't wait around to find out why, or give me time to realize I didn't suspect you of that stupid bombing at all. You simply *left*!"

T.J. closed his eyes, as if to shut out the sight of Stefanie's raw hurt. "I left because I thought you were so disappointed and disgusted, you couldn't stand the sight of me. The next day, when I came here to collect what I needed, I kept remembering the way you'd looked at me, as if I were some stranger you could never trust again. I was certain you were finished with me. I'd been offered that assignment in the north, and I'd turned it down because I hadn't wanted to be away from you, but all of a sudden it seemed like a good idea to get lost. By the time I started questioning whether you actually despised me or were just confused for a moment, it was too late. I'd committed myself to the job. And when it was over, I didn't know how to approach you. Not until Morgan went with me to that rain forest and I spilled my guts to her. When she invited me to her wedding, I jumped at the chance to be with you, Steffie."

"All of it could happen again," she said woodenly. "No matter how much I want to believe it won't, something inside me freezes up when I think about taking another gamble on us. It's the one gamble I don't seem to be up to. I love you, but I can't live with you, knowing that we're both capable of . . ." Unable to say the words again, she simply shook her head and turned away from T.J. once more.

He said nothing for a long time. There wasn't much he *could* say. The crux of the matter was that Stefanie was right: He'd walked out. He'd left her. Perhaps his sin was unforgivable, and he'd have to pay for it for the rest of his life.

Finally he made one last, desperate try. "Stefanie, do you think it was easy for me to show up at that wedding? Do you think it's been easy for me to know that I'm falling in love with you all over again, more deeply than ever, making love to you, sometimes feeling as if I've got my wife back, yet still waiting every day for you to decide whether you want me, trust me? You know that a surplus of stubborn pride is one of my many faults. Doesn't it occur to you that I wouldn't set aside that pride unless I was serious about our marriage?" He swallowed hard. "Have I been making a damn fool of myself, Steffie?"

"No," she said, without turning to face him. "I'm the damn fool."

T.J. felt his own eyes grow moist but knew there was nothing more to be said. Without making a sound he left, sick at heart, his confidence in the future completely drained.

Stefanie heard the door close. She was alone. She was cold. Empty.

It had happened again

She'd made it happen. Again.

Crawling into bed fully clothed, she curled up into a ball and pulled the covers tightly around her, trying to get warm. She couldn't. She lay shivering, wondering why the fearless Stefanie Sinclair would allow cowardice to ruin her life.

• • • •

There was another message from Ken Harmer on T.J.'s answering machine.

T.J. called Ken back and, getting Ken's machine again, tried to sound cheerful. "My machine would like to invite your machine for a beer tomorrow around five. If the machines can't make it, perhaps their owners can. The usual place. Let me know."

When he hung up, T.J. stripped off his clothes and fell into bed, wondering if he'd repeated history by leaving Stefanie instead of staying to work through the fears that were paralyzing her.

But he knew he'd had no choice but to leave. Only Stefanie could conquer her fears.

After the next day's cruise had docked, T.J. rushed home to change to jeans and a casual shirt, then went to the quiet, wood-paneled hole-in-the-wall where he and Ken Harmer had lifted many a glass over the years, a tiny bar where they could talk without competing with raucous taped music.

Ken, a sandy-haired, lanky Gary Cooper type, was seated at a corner table at the back of the room, a pitcher of beer and two glasses in front of him.

"Perfect timing," Ken said as T.J. joined him. "I just got served."

"So what's up?" T.J. asked without preamble, too tired and tense to indulge in a lot of small talk.

"Your old nemesis is out for your blood again," Ken answered, filling T.J.'s glass, then his own.

T.J. lifted his glass. "Cheers. My nemesis? You mean Bernie Dale?"

"You're a lucky man," Ken said with a grin. "You only have one nemesis."

"Bernie Dale's enough, believe me. What's going

on in his twisted little mind now? I thought Bernie had given up on me when his game with that tuna-boat scuttling didn't finish me—at least not professionally."

Ken took a swig of his beer before answering. "It seems Bernie still believes he can beat you. Now, you'll recall asking me last week to keep my eyes and ears open for anything I might stumble over about Stuart Gardner, the president of that chemical company your wife's environmental group has been hassling?"

"You've come up with something?" T.J. asked, his glass poised halfway to his lips.

"Why aren't you asking me what Gardner has to do with Bernie Dale?"

T.J. took a long pull of his beer. "Okay, what does Gardner have to do with Bernie Dale?"

Ken smiled with clear satisfaction. "Gardner just hired Bernie as a public relations flack."

"Gardner hired Bernie as his press agent? What would a chemical company want with a sleazy tabloid reporter?"

Ken sipped his beer with maddening slowness, then put the glass down and sat back in his chair, tilting it on its hind legs. "As I said, Bernie's fatal flaw is that he loves to boast. I ran into him on the street and he greeted me as if I were a long-lost friend. Asked me to go for a drink with him to celebrate his new job. When he said what it was, bells started ringing. It seemed like too much of a coincidence that Bernie was suddenly on Stuart Gardner's payroll. So I accepted Bernie's invitation, bought enough rounds to get the guy talking, and before very long hit pay dirt."

T.J.'s mind was racing. "Let me guess," he said.

"Bernie got wind of the fact that I'm working my wife's cruise as a gambler. It's common knowledge that Gardner is looking to do some kind of number on Stefanie, and since Bernie is always trying to do one on me, he went to Gardner with a proposition."

Ken nodded, not surprised by T.J.'s quick analysis of the situation. "Exactly. What Bernie told me was that he let Gardner know he'd thought of a way to make the *Bayou Belle* gambling-for-charity operation look like a scam."

"Great," T.J. said, more to himself than to Ken. "I play the part of a gambler to help Steffie and end up making more trouble for her."

"Not necessarily," Ken said cheerfully. "Forewarned is forearmed, right? Isn't that one of your favorite expressions?"

T.J. poured himself another beer and settled in to listen. "Right. So forewarn and forearm me, pal. And thanks. I owe you for this one."

Eleven

An hour later T.J. headed straight for Stefanie's place, hoping he would catch her before she went out to make the jazz club presentation on Lisa's behalf.

He entered the building along with another tenant so he didn't have to bother with the intercom, and went right up to the apartment. About to knock on the door he stopped with his hand in midair, scowling. He'd have sworn he heard a violent thunderclap, yet the sky outside had been clear when he'd entered the building.

He waited, listening.

He heard another crash of thunder, and another, then a howling wind.

T.J. pounded on Stefanie's door.

The strange noises stopped, and Stefanie opened the door.

T.J. stared at her in shock. Wearing a pale blue track suit, her hair piled on top of her head in an untidy topknot, her skin ashen, the expression in her eyes guarded, she was anything but the elegant woman he knew. Even in her shorts the day before, she'd been stylish in a casual way.

But there was something unexpectedly appealing about this Stefanie, and T.J. barely restrained himself from dragging her into his arms. "You look like a waif," he blurted.

Stefanie managed a wry smile. "Thanks."

"What's wrong?"

"Why should something be wrong?"

T.J. noticed that she wasn't meeting his eyes. "What was all the racket coming from inside the apartment?"

"What racket?"

"It sounded as if you were having your own private thunderstorm."

A flush crept over Stefanie's cheeks. "Oh . . . well, it must have been the show I was watching on television."

"You were watching some television melodrama with a storm in it?" He remembered when Stefanie had switched channels if a storm was depicted too graphically in a program.

"I guess I wasn't really watching it," she mumbled, then stood back to open the door a little wider. "Do you want to come in?"

T.J. nodded and stepped inside. He looked around. The television set wasn't on. "Why are you so pale?" he asked. "Why the strained expression? And I thought you had to make a presentation tonight."

"Why the inquisition?" she shot back. "Are you here for a reason? Did something go wrong on the cruise?"

"Nothing went wrong on the cruise, babe. But you and I need to talk. How much time do you have?"

Stefanie frowned and looked at her watch. "I'm not due at the jazz club meeting for an hour. Why do we need to talk? You mean about us?"

T.J. shook his head. "You don't have to panic, darlin'. I didn't come to talk about us. I have some information we have to discuss. Do you want to change your clothes before we go out?"

"Who says we're going out?"

T.J. sighed theatrically. "You haven't had dinner. I haven't had dinner. Let's go grab something to eat, then you can go on to your meeting."

Stefanie hesitated, then nodded. "Just give me a few minutes to freshen up and change."

"Take all the time you need, babe. I'll find something to read." With an effort, T.J. grinned and winked at Stefanie. "You don't have one of those erotic art books like your old roommate Brad keeps on his coffee table, do you?"

Stefanie managed a feeble smile and tried to tease back. "The last thing you need, T.J. Carriere, is the inspiration of erotic art."

"Thank you, ma'am. I take that remark as a compliment, I surely do."

Rolling her eyes, Stefanie hurried into the bedroom to get ready, unable to suppress her pleasure at seeing T.J., though she was certain some kind of trouble had brought him.

She dressed quickly in a navy linen business suit and white silk blouse, putting up her hair in a neat twist. Most of the members of the jazz club were men, she'd gathered, so she felt the need of a conservative, ultratailored look. Besides, a suit made her feel less vulnerable to T.J.

T.J. cleared his throat when she returned. "As always, you look great. Ready to do battle in the world of business. Maybe I should have dressed better," he added, looking down at his jeans.

"You look wonderful," Stefanie said sincerely.

"I still think there's something wrong," he said as he opened the door for her. "You seem awfully tense."

"I didn't sleep well last night, that's all."

"I'm sorry I upset you, babe. I had no right to start pushing you into something you're not ready for." He put his arm around her shoulders and gave her a quick hug. "Can we be friends again?"

Stefanie smiled. She wanted to be much more than friends with T.J., if only she could find the courage to let it happen. "Friends," she answered softly.

T.J. wasn't satisfied. He'd seen Stefanie after other sleepless nights. She'd never looked so strained. But if she didn't want to talk, he wouldn't pry.

He took her to an unpretentious diner where the hamburgers were great and the booths reasonably private. T.J. wasted no time on a slow lead-up to the situation Ken had told him about. "Babe, there's some background on that tuna-boat incident that I should have explained at the time. First, I should tell you that my picture appeared in a crummy tabloid. I was jumping off the boat just—"

"I know," Stefanie said in a small voice. "I saw it."

T.J. was stunned by the revelation. "Baby, why didn't you tell me? No wonder you suspected me of planting that bomb."

"I've asked myself a thousand times why I didn't tell you I saw that picture," she said wearily. "I still haven't come up with the answer. I think I was afraid that you wouldn't have an explanation, and by the time I knew you would, you'd left. Or maybe it's something more complex. I don't know. I can't seem to sort this one out."

T.J. was as moved by Stefanie's confusion as by her honesty. "Don't try, Steffie," he said with a tender smile. "We can sort it out together in time. For now, let's deal with our immediate problem, which is that Stuart Gardner has hired Bernie Dale as a PR man on the strength of Bernie's plan to discredit both of us."

Stefanie scowled. "Bernie Dale? Wasn't he the reporter you worked with years ago, the one who didn't let the facts get in the way of a good story? The one you blew the whistle on when he bragged to you about how he'd ruined some local businessman he didn't like, just to show he could do it?"

"You really listened to all my old stories," T.J. said fondly. "What I started to explain to you was that Bernie set me up for the tuna-boat mess. He phoned me with a tip that there was a bomb on the boat, that he wanted the story for himself but was tied up with another assignment. I didn't believe him, but I had to check it out. For once, Bernie was right about something, though he'd gotten the timing wrong. That's why I was on the boat in time to scuttle it just before the explosion. From what I can put together, Bernie heard about the bomb and saw what he hoped was an opportunity to implicate me in the sabotage, so he was skulking around the docks, ready to snap my picture and use it against me."

"The man must be crazy or stupid or both," Stefanie said, horrified. "Didn't he see all the holes in that sort of accusation?"

T.J. gave her a wry smile. "Bernie isn't brilliant, honey. He doesn't think very far ahead. And now he believes he's come up with another chance at me, one that can earn him some extra cash and maybe even enhance his lousy reputation." T.J. paused as the waiter delivered the hamburgers, then continued. "But Bernie can't resist crowing when he thinks he's about to score a point. He told me my photograph would be appearing in the tabloid, for instance. What he hadn't anticipated was that I had informed the police about his tip before I'd boarded the boat to check it out. By the time they'd arrived, the whole shootin' match was over, but I wasn't a suspect."

Stefanie nodded. "So when Bernie told you about the picture, all you had to do was mention the word libel and say the police would be your witnesses in the lawsuit?"

"Exactly, babe. I heard later that Bernie tried to get the picture pulled from the paper. He didn't manage to, but he made sure I wasn't named. And it was a lousy shot, so almost no one recognized me." T.J. shook his head. "Except you."

Stefanie stared at T.J. in shock. "Good lord, you sound like some kind of Sam Spade, carrying on an underworld existence I didn't know about."

T.J. chuckled quietly. "I guess it does seem that way. You didn't know what was going on because I had the macho idea I had to shield you from hearing about the seamy situations I sometimes got involved in. But I've learned my lesson, babe. From now on, I'll tell you everything. In the meantime, eat your burger before it gets cold."

But Stefanie had a long list of questions. She started with the one that puzzled her most at the moment. "So you think Bernie has decided to join forces with Gardner?"

"I know he has. Fortunately, he bragged about his plan to Ken Harmer."

Stefanie shook her head in confusion. "Doesn't this creep know how close you and Ken are?"

"Either he's never noticed or he's forgotten. As I said, Bernie isn't too bright. That's why he thinks he has to play all the angles. Anyway, he told Ken he'd gone to Gardner with a proposition. Just as we'd expected, babe, the intention is to send someone aboard the *Bayou Belle* who'll accuse me of cheating at cards. The story will hit the papers as a juicy scandal about another phony charity. Gardner will have his fun at your expense, and Bernie will enjoy seeing me cast as a gambling cheat."

Stefanie paled. "Oh, T.J., I'm so sorry I dragged you into this situation. Bernie will get a chance to smear your reputation because you're trying to help me."

T.J. smiled and reached across the table to take Stefanie's hand. "No wonder I love you so much, baby. Your business is being threatened and your first thought is for my reputation."

Stefanie was taken aback. What T.J. was saying was true. Important as her work was to her, it didn't come close to how much T.J. mattered. But she couldn't think about that startling realization at the moment. First things first. "What on earth are we going to do?" she asked. "Gardner has enough money to finance a dragged-out defense if we hit Bernie with a libel or a slander suit. Even if we prove Bernie's lying, the public will remember only the accusation not the truth."

T.J. grinned reassuringly at her. "The word is that tomorrow's the big day, babe. But I have a plan."

"Does it involve punching Bernie Dale in the nose?"

Laughing, T.J. shook his head. "I've left that sort of thing behind me."

"Too bad. I'm about ready to give it a try," Stefanie muttered. "But what's your plan?"

"I'm still working on it with Ken." T.J. paused, then clasped Stefanie's hand between both of his. "Baby, will you trust me to take care of this one? Just leave it with me?"

Stefanie's response was so spontaneous it surprised her as much as it did T.J. "I've trusted you to handle the Gardner problem since the day you walked into my office and showed me how to play poker," she said with a smile.

T.J. felt as if a huge weight had been lifted from his shoulders. He hadn't realized until that moment how much he needed Stefanie to believe in him. "I won't let you down, babe."

She nodded. "I know you won't, Johnny."

"You still haven't eaten your burger," he scolded, releasing her hand and trying to mask his emotions.

"I'm not very hungry."

"Eat anyway. You need your strength."

Stefanie grinned, took a few bites of her hamburger, then shook her head in despair. "You're still a bossy Cajun, T.J. Carriere."

"Always was, always will be," he said with a wink, then briefly resurrected his accent. "I gar-awn-tee." More seriously, he added, "By the way, boss lady, I need tomorrow off. Can somebody cover for me?"

"But if tomorrow's the day things are coming to a head, don't I need you on the *Bayou Belle*?"

T.J. smiled. "Babe . . ."

Stefanie nodded and laughed. "Right, Johnny. I'm to trust you."

"Well now," T.J. said to the flustered woman on the other end of the phone line, "perhaps you should tell Mr. Gardner that T.J. Carriere *insists* on seeing him this morning to pass on some information your boss will thank me for giving him. I'll be there in an hour."

"But sir—"

"One hour," T.J. repeated pleasantly, then hung up.

Exactly an hour later, dressed in a business suit, he strode into the plush, private office of the president of Gardner Chemicals.

"This better be good," Gardner muttered.

T.J. pulled up a chair, sat down, and smiled at the thin-haired, sour-faced, stocky man. "Mr. Gardner, let's start with the facts and figures my wife's environmental group has been trying to get across to you. The ones that show how you can clean up your act without cutting into your profits over the long term."

Gardner snorted. "If I was interested, I'd have seen those reports a long time ago. But I don't like a bunch of naive bleeding-hearts trying to tell me how to run my company. Unless this information you told my secretary you had for me is more important than that pile of cooked-up numbers, quit wasting my time."

T.J. kept his smile in place. "Maybe it's not more important, but perhaps it's more persuasive," he said quietly. "How much do you know about your new public relations man?"

"Bernie Dale?" Gardner leaned back in his chair, his hands clasped behind his head. "What do I need to know?"

"Just that he's a sleaze, that his credibility outside the tabloids is nonexistent." Seeing that Gardner didn't care, T.J. went straight to the point. "I'm

aware that Bernie plans to try to discredit both myself and my wife's business this afternoon with a
cooked-up scam. I know the details. Would you like
to hear them?"

Gardner sat forward abruptly. "Keep talking."

T.J. explained everything Ken had told him, then
added, "And if you don't think the local journalists
are anticipating Bernie's latest stupid move and are
ready to make mincemeat of him—and you and Gardner Chemicals—how do you suppose I found out?"

Gardner cleared his throat. "I gave no authoriza-
tion for Dale's ridiculous scheme."

T.J. pretended to believe him. "That's why I thought
you should be warned, Mr. Gardner. I know you feel
you've been treated badly by the press, but as they
say, you ain't seen nothin' yet."

With a heavy sigh, Gardner turned his swivel chair
around to stare out the window. "I'll fire Dale. I'll
disassociate myself from anything he does."

"You've already made a boner by hiring Bernie,"
T.J. pointed out. "Firing him at this point wouldn't
help. Later might be a good idea. But not just now.
When Bernie thinks he's been ill used, he gets nasty.
I know. What you have to do is turn this mess into
something positive, something that'll help your image, especially when you're trying to get approval on
that big merger you've been working on for so long."

Gardner was silent for several moments, staring
out the window. At last he spoke but didn't turn to
look at T.J. "You've done your homework," he said.
"So what are my options?"

"Well, sir," T.J. said cheerfully. "I have a plan."

Stefanie turned on the television set to catch the
news as soon as she got home from work. She'd

tried to phone T.J. several times, but had reached only his answering machine.

The national news seemed to take forever, though Stefanie half dreaded the local edition, just in case something had gone wrong on the *Bayou Belle.*

Her heart sank as the moonlike face of Stuart Gardner appeared on the screen. *Damn,* she thought, T.J. hadn't managed to ward off Bernie's attack, and the worst had happened. Gardner himself was there to be in on the kill.

She jumped up and started pacing, wondering what to do, how to get to T.J., how to make him understand that he couldn't take the blame for what was happening, that she knew he'd done what he could to protect her.

It hit her that T.J., even at this moment, was all she cared about. What an idiot she'd been! T.J. was her best friend, her lover . . . her husband. Her stubborn, sometimes quick-tempered, domineering, protective, devoted, wonderful husband. To hell with being afraid. She loved him, and she was his wife. It was time she started acting the part.

Heading for the door, planning to go to T.J. and wait outside his apartment, if necessary, Stefanie suddenly stopped in her tracks as the camera panned in on a seedy little character with ferretlike eyes and a few strands of hair plastered across an otherwise naked scalp.

The man was being pushed toward the television camera by Gardner, and Stefanie won a silent bet with herself when the name BERNIE DALE along with the words SPOKESMAN FOR GARDNER CHEMICALS were flashed on the screen over the small man's chest like numbers in a mug shot.

Stefanie swallowed hard, paralyzed with shock

while Bernie, on behalf of Stuart Gardner and Gardner Chemicals, announced the results of the company's long-term study of the proposals given them by
a local environmental group!

Stefanie turned up the volume and crouched in
front of the television screen. "Long-term study?
You refused to so much as look at that report, you
old goat," she grumbled at Gardner's image, then
realized that Bernie was saying that the changes to
the company's waste disposal methods would be im-
plemented as quickly as possible.

"T.J.," Stefanie whispered, knowing exactly who
was behind Gardner's about-face. Slowly standing
up, she was filled with pride in her husband. Without pausing to shut off the television set, Stefanie
flew out the door and down to her car.

"Where did this stupid storm come from?" she
asked irritably as rain began pelting her windshield
and thunder rolled in the distance.

There were no parking spots on the street near
T.J.'s building and none in the nearby public lot.
She had to drive three blocks before she spied a
space big enough for her little Ford, and the thought
occured to her that she might walk through the rain
only to find that T.J. was out for the evening.

She didn't care. Locking her car, she told herself a
little water wouldn't hurt her or dissolve her into a
puddle, and she could afford to sacrifice a pair of
shoes for the sake of catching T.J. the minute he
arrived home—if he did. She hoped he wouldn't make
any major detours on the way.

T.J. pulled into his reserved parking space and
got out of the car. As he walked toward the entrance

of the apartment building, he felt both elated and depressed. He'd accomplished a lot in one day: Not only was Gardner Chemicals now publicly committed to cleaning up its act, but Bernie Dale was no longer an enemy. The man had enjoyed the favorable spotlight so much, he'd decided to suggest letting bygones be bygones. To put an end to an idiotic vendetta, T.J. had shaken hands with Bernie, though he'd had to grit his teeth to do it.

What was bothering T.J. at the moment was not knowing what was ahead. Stefanie wouldn't need him as a gambler anymore, so what was his next move?

A violent explosion of thunder jarred T.J. from his reverie, and he looked up at the sky in time to see a long, jagged shaft of lightning. "Stefanie" he said, wanting to go to her.

He stood still for a moment, undecided. Was he using her fear as an excuse to get close to her again, to make her dependent on him? Or was his concern genuine?

Abruptly, he decided it was genuine. Besides, he wanted to share the day's triumph with her, even if, as he feared in the deepest part of him, it would be the last thing they shared.

"T.J.!" he heard.

Turning, he saw Stefanie running to him, her hair flattened by the rain, her flimsy cotton suit soaked, water streaming over her face. "Baby," he whispered, sure her terror had overwhelmed her at last. He started racing toward her as another crash of thunder reverberated in his ears.

To his amusement, she was laughing as she flew into his outstretched arms. "I love you!" she cried. "T.J. Carriere, will you marry me again? In a regular wedding, with our families around us and lots of champagne flowing?"

T.J. began to question his sanity—and Stefanie's. "Are you okay?" he asked, holding her close as if afraid she might be an apparition and disappear any second. "What about the storm? Is it just that you're scared?"

She laughed again and nuzzled against him. "I'm not scared. I've been working on my storm phobia, listening to tapes, watching films, even studying the physical phenomena . . . oh, who cares? I'm not afraid anymore."

T.J.'s arms tightened even more around her. "Now I understand the noises I heard when it sounded as if a hurricane had hit the interior of your apartment."

Stefanie tipped back her head to smile up at him, heedless of the rain on her face. "Our apartment, Johnny. Always ours. I was just too much of a dope to admit that it had never stopped being ours. Now, back to my question. Will you marry me? I wouldn't blame you for refusing, after everything I've put you through. But I have to warn you: I won't take no for an answer."

He was so happy it scared him. "You're not just grateful about what happened today with Gardner? Remember, I used your group's groundwork to make the man see the light, so you don't have to feel beholden or anything."

"Gardner didn't have the time of day for that groundwork until you got to him," Stefanie said, then reached up to cradle T.J.'s face between her two hands. "Yes, I'm grateful to you, but not *just* grateful or beholden. I'm also crazy about you, and proud of you, and I can't wait to hear the details of today's momentous happenings. I'll have you know, however, that I was on my way to propose to you before I knew what you'd managed to do."

T.J. began to believe what was happening enough to tease a little. "You do remember I still have one poker chip left on your marker, don't you, Stefanie? Yes, I'll marry you, but aren't you worried about how I might decide to collect on that chip once you're back in my clutches?"

"I'm terrified," she shot back. "And if you ever call me Stefanie again instead of the lovely endearments you usually use, I'll . . ."

"You'll what?" T.J. said, laughing as happiness filled his whole being. He lifted his wife in his arms to carry her to his car and take her home where they both belonged. "Aren't you afraid of our fights anymore, darlin'?"

Twining her arms around his neck, Stefanie shook her head vehemently. "I'm not the least bit afraid of them, Johnny."

"You're sure?" he asked, raising one brow as he flashed his most wicked grin at her.

Stefanie smiled and brought her lips close to T.J.'s ear. "Baby," she whispered, "I gar-awn-tee."

Don't miss Lisa Sinclair's love story in _The Dreamweavers:_ SOPHISTICATED LADY
LOVESWEPT #379
February 1990
(on sale in January 1990)

THE EDITOR'S CORNER

This month our color reflects the copper leaves of autumn, and we hope when a chill wind blows, you'll curl up with a LOVESWEPT. In keeping with the seasons, next month our color will be the deep green of a Christmas pine, and our books will carry a personalized holiday message from the authors. You'll want to collect all six books just because they're beautiful—but the stories are so wonderful, even wrapped in plain brown paper they'd be appealing!

Sandra Brown is a phenomenon! She never disappoints us. In **A WHOLE NEW LIGHT,** LOVESWEPT #366, Sandra brings together two special people. Cyn McCall desperately wants to shake up her life, but when Worth Lansing asks her to spend the weekend with him in Acapulco, she's more than a little surprised—and tempted. Worth had always been her buddy, her friend, her late husband's business partner. But what will happen when Cyn sees him in a whole new light?

Linda Cajio's gift to you is a steamy, sensual romance: **UNFORGETTABLE,** LOVESWEPT #367. Anne Kitteridge and James Farraday also know each other. In fact, they've known each other all their lives. Anne can't forget how she'd once made a fool of herself over James. And James finds himself drawn once again to the woman who was his obsession. When James stables his prize horse at Anne's breeding farm, they come together under the most disturbingly intimate conditions, and there's no way they can deny their feelings. As always Linda creates an emotionally charged atmosphere in this unforgettable romance.

(continued)

Courtney Henke's first LOVESWEPT, **CHA-MELEON,** was charming, evocative, and tenderly written, and her second, **THE DRAGON'S REVENGE,** LOVESWEPT #368 is even more so. J.D. Smith is instantly captivated by Charly, the woman he sees coaching a football team of tough youths, and he wonders what it would be like to tangle with the woman her players call the Dragon Lady. He's met his match in Charly—in more ways than one. When he teaches her to fence, they add new meaning to the word touché.

Joan Elliott Pickart will cast a spell over you with **THE MAGIC OF THE MOON,** LOVESWEPT #369. She brings together Declan Harris, a stressed-out architect, and Joy Barlow, a psychologist, under the rare, romantic light of a blue moon—and love takes over. Declan cherishes Joy, but above all else she wants his respect—the one thing he finds hardest to give. Joan comes through once more with a winning romance.

LOVESWEPT #370, **POOR EMILY** by Mary Kay McComas is not to be missed. The one scene sure to make you laugh out loud is when Emily's cousin explains to her how finding a man is like choosing wallpaper. It's a scream! Mary Kay has a special touch when it comes to creating two characters who are meant to be together. Emily falls for Noble, the hero, even before she meets him, by watching him jog by her house every day. But when they do meet, Emily and Noble find they have lots more in common than ancestors who fought in the Civil War—and no one ever calls her Poor Emily again.

Helen Mittermeyer begins her *Men of Ice* series
(continued)

with **QUICKSILVER,** LOVESWEPT #371. Helen is known for writing about strong, dangerous, enigmatic men, and hero Piers Larraby is all of those things. When gorgeous, silver-haired Damiene Belson appears from the darkness fleeing her pursuers, Piers is her sanctuary in the storm. But too many secrets threaten their unexpected love. You can count on Helen to deliver a dramatic story filled with romance.

Don't forget to start your holiday shopping early this year. Our LOVESWEPT Golden Classics featuring our Hometown Hunk winners are out in stores right now, and in the beginning of November you can pick up our lovely December LOVE-SWEPTs. They make great gifts. What could be more joyful than bringing a little romance into someone's life?

Best wishes,
Sincerely,

Carolyn Nichols

Carolyn Nichols
   Editor
LOVESWEPT
Bantam Books
666 Fifth Avenue
New York, NY 10103

FAN OF THE MONTH

Tricia Smith

I'm honored to have been chosen as a "fan of the month" for LOVESWEPT. A mother of two children with a house full of animals, I've been a romance reader for years. I was immediately captivated when I read the first LOVESWEPT book, **HEAVEN'S PRICE** by Sandra Brown. Ms. Brown is a very compelling author, along with so many of the authors LOVESWEPT has introduced into my life.

Each month I find myself looking forward to new adventures in reading with LOVESWEPT. The story lines are up-to-date, very well researched, and totally enthralling. With such fantastic authors as Iris Johansen, Kay Hooper, Fayrene Preston, Kathleen Creighton, Joan Elliott Pickart, and Deborah Smith, I'm always enchanted, from cover to cover, month after month.

I recently joined the Gold Coast Chapter of Romance Writers of America and have made wonderful friends who are all well-known authors as well as just great people. I hope to attend an RWA convention someday soon in order to meet the authors who've enriched my life in so many ways. Romance reading for me is not a pasttime but a passion.

THE DELANEY DYNASTY

Men and women whose loves an passions are so glorious
it takes many great romance novels by three bestselling
authors to tell their tempestuous stories.

THE SHAMROCK TRINITY

☐	21975	RAFE, THE MAVERICK *by Kay Hooper*	$2.95
☐	21976	YORK, THE RENEGADE *by Iris Johansen*	$2.95
☐	21977	BURKE, THE KINGPIN *by Fayrene Preston*	$2.95

THE DELANEYS OF KILLAROO

☐	21872	ADELAIDE, THE ENCHANTRESS *by Kay Hooper*	$2.75
☐	21873	MATILDA, THE ADVENTURESS *by Iris Johansen*	$2.75
☐	21874	SYDNEY, THE TEMPTRESS *by Fayrene Preston*	$2.75

THE DELANEYS: *The Untamed Years*

☐	21899	GOLDEN FLAMES *by Kay Hooper*	$3.50
☐	21898	WILD SILVER *by Iris Johansen*	$3.50
☐	21897	COPPER FIRE *by Fayrene Preston*	$3.50

Buy them at your local bookstore or use this page to order.

NEW!
Handsome Book Covers Specially Designed To Fit Loveswept Books

Our new French Calf Vinyl book covers come in a set of three great colors— royal blue, scarlet red and kachina green.

Each 7" × 9½" book cover has two deep vertical pockets, a handy sewn-in bookmark, and is soil and scratch resistant.

To order your set, use the form below.

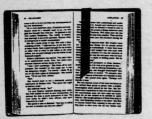

Special Offer
Buy a Bantam Book
for only 50¢.

Now you can have Bantam's catalog filled with hundreds of titles plus take advantage of our unique and exciting bonus book offer. A special offer which gives you the opportunity to purchase a Bantam book for only 50¢. Here's how!

By ordering any five books at the regular price per order, you can also choose any other single book listed (up to a $5.95 value) for just 50¢. Some restrictions do apply, but for further details why not send for Bantam's catalog of titles today!

Just send us your name and address and we will send you a catalog!